Beyond This Life

BEYOND THIS LIFE

A Novel
by
Greg Stone

PINK UNICORN

PUBLISHING

Greg Stone is a commercial mediator and non-profit founder, as well as a spiritual seeker. In addition to writing fiction, he has written non-fiction books on faith-based reconciliation and peacemaking.

Pink Unicorn Publishing, Westlake Village 91361
© 2020 Pink Unicorn Publishing
All rights reserved. Published 2020

ISBN: 978-1-7353685-1-1

Based on the novel *Under the Tree* by Greg Stone
© Pink Unicorn Publishing 2004

Published in the United States of America

Dedicated to those
who have discovered their true nature
as an immortal soul.

1

The Explorer's tires hit a patch of ice hidden beneath a fresh dusting of snow. The SUV lost traction. Ray Carte, accustomed to wintry conditions, corrected. The vehicle skidded. Ray corrected again, but he was too late. Physics had taken over: the ice was too slick and the momentum too great. The Explorer spun out of control. Gravity pitched in and the vehicle hurtled down a snow-covered incline.

That would have been the end of the story—if not for the sacrifice of a small tree. Though the impact shattered its bark, the pine remained standing, holding the weight of the Explorer, which shuddered twice before its engine cut out.

Blood streamed down Ray's forehead. The last thing he saw before he passed out was a toy monk dangling from the rearview mirror, rocking back and forth as though praying.

Tranquility blanketed the snow-covered mountain pass.

Two hours later, a Rocky Mountain Rescue team clambered down the slope, walkie-talkies crackling with commands. The rescuers disassembled the wreckage with crowbars and power saws. They pried Ray's limp body from behind the wheel.

"Get him out of here. Move it," the lead climber shouted as rescuers scrambled up the rocky incline and hoisted the body into a Bell Jet Ranger for the flight to intensive care.

Ray's pulse barely registered a beat.

2

Officer Ernie Lesco of the Jefferson County Sheriff's Department walked into the intensive care unit and hefted a plastic evidence bag filled with Ray's belongings onto the counter of the nurse's station.

Head Nurse Lani Clare looked up with a smile at the officer's frost bitten cheeks, "Looks like someone could use a hot cup of coffee."

"Or a warm bed," Officer Ernie said, shaking off the chill.

"No vacancies," Nurse Lani joked. "You'll have to settle for a coffee."

"It's a nightmare out there."

"Not much better in here," Lani replied.

"You don't suppose our patient could answer a few questions?"

"Not unless you're a medium. Not likely he's going to make it. We don't even have an ID yet."

"Ray Carte," Ernie said, pointing at the evidence bag. "Thirty-five years old."

Lani rifled through the bag and removed a driver's license

from the new patient's wallet. She scanned the vital statistics.

"Half an inch short of six feet," she declared. "A near miss." She recalled wheeling the bruised and swollen body from ER up to the ICU. "It's a damn shame. He must have been a handsome fellow before the wreck."

Office Ernie watched on as she input data into a computer. The patient weighed a hundred and seventy five pounds. Muscle tone was excellent. He was fit, which tipped the scales toward recovery. Of course, there were things one was not supposed to do to a body—like driving it off a cliff and slamming it into a tree.

Officer Ernie circled behind the counter. Pointing to the victim's phone he said, "His password might be his birthday."

She copied the patient's birthdate from his license into the password prompt. Success. She searched the "recent call" list. Two names appeared more than a dozen times: Randi Carte and Chase Callahan. She reached Randi on the first ring.

After a brief conversation, she hung up and briefed Ernie. "His mother. She'll catch the next plane out from Los Angeles. In the meantime, she'll to try to locate her ex-husband."

"Anyone local on that list?" Ernie asked.

"I'll keep trying." Lani dialed the second name on the list—Chase Callahan—and repeated the same conversation almost verbatim. Officer Ernie smiled. She had obviously mastered the art of breaking bad news.

"His girlfriend," Lani said as she hung up. "She'll be here soon."

"I'll be downstairs in the cafeteria. Let me know when they show up." Ernie stowed his accident report clipboard and ambled to the elevator, continuing to shake off the bitter cold that threatened to settle into his bones.

* * *

An hour later, Chase stared down at Ray's lifeless body. The first glance was brutal. She barely recognized his face, now drained of color. His bruised and bandaged form sprouted arterial lines, catheters, endotracheal tubes, and IVs. She steadied herself against the side rail of the bed as a spell of dizziness washed over her.

Nurse Lani guided her to a chair next to the head of Ray's bed. "Make yourself comfortable. I'll be right outside."

"I was always the optimistic one," Chase blurted out. She winced, with embarrassment. She knew she wasn't making sense.

To her relief, Lani looked back from the doorway with a sympathetic smile. "No reason to stop being optimistic."

Chase closed her eyes and took a deep breath, trying to calm her racing heart. In the past, when Ray was troubled, she was the one that offered encouragement and problem-solving insights. Her flashes of intuition no longer mattered—you could not share a bright idea with someone in a coma.

There was something else she couldn't share: *she was pregnant.* She had found out only a little over a week ago. The first time the test strip had turned blue she had laughed—a mistake, for sure. The second time, she'd had a minor panic attack. Then the result came back positive for the third day in a row. She had spent the rest of the week in a sleepless terror, wondering how Ray would react. Now she might never know.

The heart monitor beat out a steady rhythm, echoing against the bare walls of the hospital room. Chase settled into the chair next to Ray's battered body and tried to steady her nerves. She clasped Ray's hand. She was not used to losing her composure, and she did not want to start now.

She leaned over and whispered in Ray's ear. "Baby, I just want you to know I'm here. I don't know if you can hear me, but we'll get through this together. I know you're strong. And I'm not going anywhere."

With a brave smile, she squeezed Ray's hand and let her head drop onto his sleeping body. Before long, she was fast asleep. Fear and adrenaline had taken its toll.

* * *

Hours later Randi Carte arrived. Head Nurse Lani dropped her professional demeanor and welcomed her with a hug. Their eyes locked for a brief moment, but it was long enough for them to share the empathy reserved for mothers who know the meaning of fear. In this situation, the hug meant more than token words of encouragement.

"I wasn't able to reach Ray's father. Haven't spoken with him in years. To be honest, I don't even know if the poor man is alive. I can't say I care much, but I wanted him to know about the accident."

"Don't worry. At least you're here. Let's go see your son. I must warn you, it was a pretty severe accident."

Randi tensed. *Was Ray's condition worse than she had assumed*? When she entered Ray's room, the sight of Ray's comatose body shook her confidence. The presence of a strange woman napping at Ray's side also gave her pause.

"This is Chase Callahan," Lani said, attempting to lessen the mystery. *Did they know each other*? she wondered.

Chase awoke with a startle, disoriented and groggy.

Randi extended her hand, "I'm Ray's mother, Randi. Randi Carte."

"Oh, of course. I'm sorry, I was—"

"You must be his girlfriend."

Chase met her eyes and shook her hand with a steady grip. "Fiancé."

Randi studied the younger woman, Ray's "fiancé." She noted that she wore her hair in a simple cut, flattering but unpretentious, and her brown eyes flecked with green were unwavering.

Chase watched as Randi shuffled to her son's bed, fluffed the pillows, and smoothed the sheets. Ray had said little about his mother. In that void, Chase had imagined a dour housewife devoid of humor. Instead, she encountered a robust, warm woman with a Southern California tan, radiant in the middle of winter. She had her fair share of wrinkles, but they were the result of too much sun rather than drudgery and stress. Her warm, mothering gestures surprised Chase.

"Ray told me about you," Randi said after she had tidied up her son's bed.

"I hope it was all good."

"Said he was seeing a new girl. But then again, he's said that before."

Chase laughed. She appreciated Randi's bluntness as much as her warmth.

"You're different though," Randi said as she took a seat next to Chase.

"How so?" Chase leaned in closer, intrigued.

"Oh, you know. Often they were… blond. To be honest, my hopes of wedding bells and grandchildren faded long ago." It was a sly question as much as a statement.

"Ah, yes." Chase replied with a knowing smile. She realized that Ray inherited his frankness from his mother. Not the type to hide his past out of pride, he had shared with her tales of his bachelor life. They had enjoyed skimming through old photo albums, laughing at his bad haircuts and old flings.

"He'll be fine. I know it." Randi sighed. "He's one tough cookie."

Chase had always considered herself to be strong. Now she knew she had met her match.

"There's always hope," Randi continued when Chase failed to reply.

"Perhaps not," said Dr. Sloane, as he entered. He was the neurosurgeon in charge of Ray's care.

Both women turned abruptly, startled.

"What did you just say?" Chase blurted out.

The doctor zeroed in on Randi. "You're the mother?"

"I am," she said, dropping any pretense of warmth.

"Your son suffered severe injuries," he went on. "Hemorrhagic contusions in the interior frontal and temporal lobes. We see these often in vehicle accidents."

He pinched Ray above the collarbone: no reaction.

Randi flinched. While she hadn't expected the doctor to inflate false hopes, his manner seemed unnecessarily brusque.

"Yes, but he's alive," Chase retorted.

"Our main concern," Sloane continued, "is swelling. A patient can recover from the original injury, but secondary injury due to swelling can be fatal. The ICP—"

Sloane stopped short, reading Randi's confusion tinged with anger. He also noted Chase's displeasure—she seethed with barely concealed contempt. Recognizing he had crossed a line—after all these were not residents accustomed to his gruff manner—he started over. "We inserted a tube into his brain to monitor pressure and drain fluid. The intracranial pressure is in the mid-twenties. Not ideal. We'll do everything we can. I just don't want to seem overly optimistic. I don't want to convey false hope. It's one day at a time."

Before either Randi or Chase could collect their thoughts and ask a question, Sloane was gone, a master of the magician's quick entrance and exit.

Nurse Lani followed him out, miming a frown and mouthing an apology.

"He has to be realistic. I guess." She sought to excuse the doctor's behavior.

"He didn't have to be a jerk," Randi shot back.

Chase wiped away an involuntary tear. Stunned by the prognosis, they let the news sink in as they watched Ray's chest barely rise and fall. Randi broke the silence. "I brought him into the world without so much as a thought. Now..." Her voice trailed off.

"You know," Chase started. "I haven't told Ray yet, but—"

She stopped in midsentence. Now was not the time to break the news. It was too soon. They had only just met. She had no idea how Randi would react to her pregnancy. *That's alright, she thought. I can carry this burden. Alone.*

"What?" Randi pried.

"Huh? I don't remember," Chase mumbled, sinking back into her chair. She did not have the strength to improvise a clever lie.

Moments later, Officer Ernie entered, juggling a large coffee and his clipboard. Unlike the medical staff, his expression remained upbeat, as if he were accustomed to battling tragedy with a wry sense of humor.

"I have a lot of respect for the human spirit," he informed Chase and Randi. "You can look at someone... But you can't tell, just by looking at them, if they're gonna pull through. Nope. Stuff happens we don't see. If you know what I mean."

Chase wondered if Lani had sent Ernie, knowing he would cheer them up. She managed a weak smile as she studied Ray. In her mind, she could hear him sharpening his intellectual sword. They had often talked late into the night about "stuff that no one sees." On those evenings, they would linger around the kitchen table to discuss questions of life after death. They would playfully opine on the meaning of human life. Ray, an avid materialist, struggled with spiritual views.

He always managed to dig up rational explanations to defeat any supernatural claims she advanced.

Chase countered Ray's skepticism with good humor. For her, sparring with Ray was a diversion and a way to strengthen their relationship; but, for Ray, debate was serious business. He had a PhD in the philosophy of science and he was not about to let a weak argument or flippant remark go unchallenged. Chase rarely pushed the conversation beyond the point of civility. She would concede at just the right moment. At this moment she wondered—would he endorse Dr. Sloane's harsh realism or Officer Ernie's idealistic optimism?

"To your knowledge," Ernie broke in, "has Ray ever been in an accident before?"

Chase glanced up.

"Not that I know of," she replied.

An exhaustive interrogation followed. Was Ray "given to drink"? Did he have a temper? Did he have any enemies? Were his financial affairs in order? Recently, had anyone threatened him?

Officer Ernie asked each question as if he was solving a parlor mystery. The game might be worth playing, Chase thought, if Ray magically came back to life the minute they discovered "whodunit." Unfortunately, the mystery remained unsolved. Ernie returned his pencil to the clasp of his clipboard and shook his head.

Randi had remained silent during most the interview, but now she chimed in. "What happened, exactly? Can you tell us?"

Ernie sipped his coffee and then mumbled something about Mother Nature turning nasty.

"What was that?" Randi asked, as if she were correcting an insolent schoolboy.

"Ice," he said. "It was mainly the ice. The conditions. Of course, we won't really know until the young man is able to talk."

Promising he would return when the moment of recovery arrived, Ernie tipped his hat and made his escape, leaving the two women to sort through the silence that followed. As soon as they were alone, Randi resumed her vigil over Ray's sleeping form, leaving Chase alone to wonder: *what had happened up on that mountain?*

3

The winding path climbed a slope and crested over a rise, then carved its way through a meadow dappled with vibrant yellow and purple wildflowers. In the thin mountain air, the hiker's pulse thumped in his cranium, the product of a heart gone mad in its attempt to deliver oxygen to the brain.

As he slowed his pace and let his lungs fill, a stray thought crossed his mind—he had forgotten something, possibly something important. He had a vague impression that he was supposed to deliver a message, but he had no idea what that message might have been. He figured it would come to him eventually; it always did.

Before he could sort out his faulty memory, he saw her— she was sitting cross-legged under a tree at the far end of the meadow. The sculpted folds of her diaphanous blue dress pooled about her. Her hair was pulled back, framing a pale face set off by strikingly intense blue eyes. He studied this peculiar figure, so out of place on this remote hillside, and imagined for a moment that he had wandered into Wonder-land and had stumbled upon Alice. Her face was placid. Her eyes took in everything and nothing at the same time. If she was aware of his presence, she gave no indication.

Ray crossed the meadow, keeping to the trail that wound past the tree under which the unusual young woman was seated. As he neared her position, he slowed to a shuffle. Something about her captivated him. He was on the verge of calling out a greeting but, instead, he obeyed an unwritten rule: when a hiker encounters another hiker on the trail, he shall respect the sanctity of solitude. Anything more than a quiet greeting or nod was frowned upon. His curiosity and her striking appearance tempted him to break the rule, but prudence prevailed and he maintained mountain etiquette. As he came upon her position, he nodded briefly and quickened his pace.

"You're not on the path," she said, cordially.

He glanced down, and then challenged her assertion. "I've not been trampling the flowers, if that's what you mean."

"Not that path, silly," she said, flashing a patronizing smile.

"Ah, *that* path." It was his turn to patronize.

He wondered if she was part of a local commune, a remnant of the sixties when hippies, spiritual seekers, and social utopians flooded these foothills. The scene had died out years ago, but sporadic attempts to resurrect the era were not uncommon. Perhaps the young lady under the tree was part of the latest such effort.

"How do you know I'm not on the path?" Ray asked.

"You're not ready. I can see *that*," she said as she rose to her feet. "Sorry, I've interrupted your journey. Have a good day."

Her taunt, delivered with a sweet smile, got under his skin.

Still, he responded politely, "I don't mind the interruption. I want to know what you see. *Why* am I not ready?"

"Didn't mean to hurt your feelings," she replied. "Just an observation, that's all."

So, she was going to be evasive, coy rather than direct. He wanted to deflate her pride, but how? Wilt her arrogance with blistering sarcasm? Turn his back and walk away? Both strategies might close the door on his ability to learn her identity.

"Do you belong to a cult?" he asked, opting for a blunt approach. "Are you someone who meditates, trying to get out of their head? Is that it?"

Alice's observation—that he was not ready for the spiritual path—hit a raw nerve. *It was her attitude*, he realized. Some believers conveyed their observations as though only holy water touched their lips.

"I've upset you," she said. "And I've ruined your pilgrimage. And all you wanted was escape from obnoxious people shoving their way through shallow lives."

"You didn't ruin a thing," Ray said. "I'm not escaping from anyone. In fact, I was amusing myself, imagining you were Alice—"

"Alice?"

"The girl in Wonderland."

Something about her sweet exterior crowned with a smile was maddening. Did it convey scorn or amusement? He couldn't tell.

"Either that or the Evil Queen," he said. "I'm not sure just yet."

"Well, it's true, you're *not* ready, are you?"

He looked for the humor in her words, found none, and ended up wondering if her words were meant to wound. He might have responded with an angry outburst, if it weren't for his nagging feeling that he'd forgotten something. He had no time to waste arguing with a stranger. Why, then, was it was so hard for him to disengage from the banter and get on with his hike?

"I've given a fair amount of thought to spiritual matters," he said. "Life is more than beer and pretzels. Compassion. That's the secret, right? We must learn to be still and listen, with our hearts." Giving up any pretense of politeness, he said, "I'll admit I haven't pulled out the Ouija board lately. And I don't run up bills phoning the Psychic Hotline. I don't have a guru to tell me when to breathe."

"Then we'll get along," she replied. "We're both realists. Though reality may not be what you think it is."

"Oh? You know this? And I'm not ready?"

"I suppose." She prepared to leave. First, she issued a challenge, "Are you saying you've given some thought to spiritual matters?"

"No need to be surprised," he replied.

"Then you know you're a spirit, right? Not a body."

"I'm not into idle speculation, but I do live a spiritual life—"

"I don't get it." She flashed an exaggerated look of puzzlement. "How can one live a spiritual life if one is not a spirit?"

"They've shown spirit doesn't exist."

"Who's shown *that*?" She gaped with disbelief. It was as if she was prodding and antagonizing him on purpose, but why? Was she seeking an emotional reaction? Did she enjoy watching other people squirm?

"Scientists," Ray said in his calmest voice. "You know—"

"No, I don't know. I'm disappointed. I thought you were a realist."

Again, she had rubbed a hot nerve. Now he couldn't let go. Fearing she would walk away before he could score another point, he shot back. "Science is real, sweetheart. It's what is real. Not—"

"Spirit? If so, then you cannot be spiritual. That's only logical." She winked.

He wanted to return the volley with lighthearted banter, but, searching within, he could not find the spirit of play. The persistent feeling that he had forgotten something important was only getting stronger.

"If you're not a spirit, you must be a robot." Her soft voice was cutting. "A nice robot, a polite robot, but a robot nonetheless."

"Forget it," he cut her off. *This wasn't going anywhere.* Alice had crawled down too many rabbit holes and had chased too many mad hatters. Besides, she seemed a dozen years younger than him. He was debating with a child.

She walked away. She disappeared behind the birch trees, reappeared, and then disappeared again. Without warning Ray was overcome by panic-induced nausea. Why was his head pounding? What had he forgotten? Come to think of it, he could not even remember driving to the trailhead. A voice echoed, seemingly out of his past: "*Get him out of here. Let's move it.*" He looked up, expecting to see a helicopter, but only found a swiftly darkening sky.

More than anything, Ray realized he didn't want "Alice" to leave. He feared being alone. He had an impulse to sprint after her, but his legs seemed frozen. In all his years of hiking, he had never lost his nerve, but now…

Then he heard her voice from the distance. "So next time we meet we will talk about spirit?"

"Next time? What shall I call you?" he shouted.

"Alice is fine."

"I'm Ray. Ray Carte. Wait. Wait for me."

4

Three tanned and weathered young men dressed in hiking boots, jeans, and Patagonia pullovers, slipped quietly into Ray's room. They nodded to Chase and then fixed their collective gaze on Ray's immobile body. Chase recognized the men. They were rock climbers—adrenaline freaks who risked their lives crawling up granite walls like spiders armed with pitons. Ray had joined them on dozens of ascents.

The climbers eschewed chitchat: stony silence framed their contemplation. The sight of a climbing partner plugged into life-support packed the wallop of a heavyweight's uppercut. The Mountain had beaten one of them, even if the battle had not taken place on a climb. With their mortality on trial, they shuffled out, having paid their respects.

Minutes later, Chase's sister, Eva, delivered hot coffee and deli sandwiches. Bren, her daughter, tiptoed behind her. Hospital rules forbade minors in ICU, but that directive was one that Nurse Lani had never liked. Instead of playing bouncer, she preoccupied herself with Ray's chart and watched Bren out of the corner of her eye. She looked about ten, seemed alert and intelligent—precocious but not a troublemaker.

As Chase introduced Randi and briefed her sister on the unsettling medical prognosis, Bren slipped free of her mother's iron grip. Leaning over Ray, she offered her frank appraisal: "He's gone, isn't he?"

"Bren!" Eva grabbed her daughter's hand and pulled her close.

"But, Mom, he looks so—"

"I'm so sorry," Eva said with a quick yank on Bren's hand. "She hasn't quite learned to filter her comments yet. Maybe we need a little lunch break, huh sweetie?"

Chase and Randi shared understanding nods as they hugged and kissed Eva, who continued to pepper her exit with profuse apologies.

* * *

At eleven o'clock, the graveyard shift signed on. Silence fell over the halls. Chase, emotionally exhausted, could hear only the shuffling of nurse's feet as she curled up in her chair next to Ray. Randi searched a closet, found a pillow, and propped it up behind Chase's head. Chase smiled, snuggled her face into the soft linen and dozed off.

Randi took the remaining seat, wrapped her fingers around her son's cold hand and whispered, "Ray? Can you hear me? Ray?"

The stiff ghostly pallor of his features reminded her of a

time long ago. She had been nine when her Aunt Katherine had passed. At the wake, she had found herself transfixed by Aunt K's body as it lay on display for mourners paying their last respects. She had glanced around the room. The mourners, lost in their grief, had not seemed to pay much attention to Randi, the youngster in the group. With a trembling hand, she had reached out and touched Auntie K's cold wrist—her first encounter with death. The sight of Randi's tiny hand on the corpse had shocked her poor mother's delicate nerves. With a gasp, her mother had whisked her out of the funeral home. She remembered wanting to ask someone why Aunt K was there and yet… *not there.* She had tried, but the dreadful silence that filled the car on the way home had served as warning—she was to remain silent.

Now, all these years later, as she looked down at Ray, she experienced the same epiphany: *Something was missing— this was not her son.* That which made Ray *who he was* had vanished. It wasn't that his body had run down like an old machine and quit working. No, *something* had gone missing. The only difference, she assured herself, was that Ray, unlike Auntie K, was coming back.

Randi heard the door open behind her and then heard a whisper, "Can I speak with you for a moment?"

Randi looked up and saw a man wearing a black suit with a priest's collar.

"Father James McCarty, hospital chaplain. The kind nurse told me you were the patient's mother."

Randi, still surprised at the arrival of a priest, barely nodded. Father McCarty extended his hand and motioned toward the door with a wink and a smile so warm it could melt the heart of a barbarian. The priest's affable demeanor promised comfort, so she followed him outside into the hall.

"I heard Dr. Sloane wasn't overly optimistic," McCarty said when the door to Ray's room had closed behind them.

Randi was surprised. McCarty was a straight shooter. He wasn't offering watered-down platitudes.

"A bit pessimistic," she said, cringing at the thought of the unpleasant encounter. "Didn't want to get my hopes up."

"As long as he didn't kill your hopes. Hope, I always say, is the glue that keeps life together. Kill a person's hope and you might as well kill them."

A single tear welled up in Randi's eye. She glanced up to find Father McCarty studying her.

"You're wondering about my faith," she said.

"A little curious. It's my business. I don't know if I can help but I did want to take your spiritual pulse."

"My spiritual pulse? Do you propose a diagnosis?" she asked.

"The prognosis is good—as long as you're allowed to confront your doubts."

"Doubts?"

"Do you believe in an afterlife?" he asked. The warmth that emanated from his kind smile was tangible.

"I don't... I just don't know."

"I don't either," he said.

Randi laughed. Father McCarty reminded her of the sharp-tongued old priests who used to shuffle hurriedly out of St. Benedict's Catholic Church in her childhood neighborhood. They always seemed in a hurry to save souls with a twinkle in their eye.

"While I don't know—in the sense of possessing physical evidence," he went on, "I *know*. While I can't take you there, I know. I know in the way we know inside. That won't win debates, but it's what we must turn to… when we are forced to make decisions."

"Decisions?" she asked.

"They may ask you to make a decision about your son's care." McCarty looked Randi in the eye as he spoke.

"You mean *the* decision—"

"—to terminate life support. *If* the time comes, it makes a difference how we see our actions. If we believe in an afterlife, we might see it one way. If not, we may see it in another light."

"To be honest, I don't know. In some ways, the decision has already been made. I look at Ray… something's different."

"We call it the empty vessel." He paused. His evaluation had been more forthright than he had intended.

She gestured for him to continue.

"Clergy, like myself, tend to the spiritual aspects of life. But, when it comes to these situations, we see the same empty vessel you see. We should see more, but we don't. When we approach the door leading to the Other Side, we find it closed."

Empty vessel, Randi mused. That was exactly what she had witnessed with Auntie K years ago.

"If you could open that door and see beyond this life, I guess that would make you a medium," she said, more to herself than to Father McCarty.

He flustered.

"That isn't kosher, is it?" she said with smile.

McCarty returned the smile. At least she had a sense of humor, an invaluable possession in difficult times. Take my earthly possessions and I'll be okay, he had always told himself, but if you steal my sense of humor, I'm finished.

"The seminary didn't teach us how to become mediums, but sometimes I think they should have. For the most part, we're working in the dark."

"Most of us work in the dark," Randi said as she looked up and down the deserted halls of the Intensive Care Unit.

"That's when we depend on our faith," he said.

Hope was one thing, faith quite another, Randi thought. She recalled the year following her divorce. For the first time since she was a girl, she had joined a congregation. At that time, she wasn't sure if she was looking for answers or for a support group, but she had nurtured a vague hope that religion would help her put the pieces of her life back together again. However, she had found nothing but a dry hole. Perhaps it was because she had trouble believing in something she could not see or touch.

"I'm not particularly strong in the faith department," she said, summing up her reflections for Father McCarty. "If I don't know something, I leave it be."

"Seems like you're confusing faith with blind faith. There's a time for that, I suppose. But that isn't the only kind of faith—"

"Why are we kept in the dark?" she broke in. "If heaven

exists, why the big mystery? That doesn't figure. There's no logic to it."

"Given that I've been hired to vouch for heaven, you'd think I would have been given a tour," the priest replied with a self-deprecating smile. "Hard to sell the cruise when you haven't been on the ship."

"Maybe we're not supposed to know the destination until we arrive. That's what I tell myself. But when it's someone else… it's hard. That's the mother in me talking."

"Many of us Fathers wrestle with the same questions."

"Any answers?"

"Holding hands helps."

He cradled her hands in his.

"There's another kind of faith," he said, returning to his earlier point. "An affirmative and creative faith. Has to do with the exercise of free will. We may not control God's creation, but we can exercise our endowed free will. We're not helpless debris floating on a sea of uncertainty. We decide how to respond to life's challenges. Maybe that's why we're here. Maybe we're here to learn to exercise that free will."

"Maybe," she said, unconvinced. She closed her eyes and tried to conjure up an affirmative prayer, but it wasn't there. She thanked Father McCarty with a look and withdrew her hands.

"I know you'd prefer a kosher medium, but, if you don't find one, I'll look in on you from time to time." McCarty tossed her a departing wink as he exited.

Randi returned to her bedside vigil with a heavy heart. Previously, she had busied herself with practical concerns, but Father McCarty's candor had pushed her to a deeper appreciation of the situation. Her bubble of adrenaline-fueled optimism had burst; she was left facing stark reality. She touched Ray's wrist, as she had touched Auntie K so many years ago, and searched her heart for a sign of Father McCarty's elusive faith.

5

Ray called out after Alice. "Wait!"

She didn't look back. A few seconds later, she disappeared into a grove of trees, her blue dress flowing like a master's brush stroke past the white birch, which sparkled with the afterglow of a fading sun. Ray gave chase and reached the trees behind which she had disappeared. Beyond the birch grove, a wall of stately pines reached up and disappeared into low clouds that blanketed the forest.

He wasn't sure why he needed to find Alice. He was not afraid of being alone in the woods. Rather, it seemed she held a clue to a nagging mystery. She possessed answers to questions he had not yet formulated. Driven by curiosity he ran deep into the dense woods, through wispy tendrils of fog that morphed into ghostly apparitions.

Picking up his pace, he hurdled past fallen branches and rotted stumps, barely maintaining his footing on the damp pine needles. The orange rays of the setting sun lit the forest on fire. Ray noticed he was shivering. He tried to jog his memory. *How did he get here? Where was his car? Where had he been just before he encountered Alice?*

At exactly the moment he tried to place the missing time, an odd sense of looming terror arose. He figured he must keep moving forward, so he pressed on. With careful steps he navigated past another dense thicket of twisted branches and made a discovery—the forest opened up into a pastoral clearing. In the center stood a rustic cabin. Light spilled from the windows.

The cabin was inviting, yet Ray felt something was not right. Glancing back toward the forest, he considered retracing his steps, but it was too late. Darkness had already descended. In spite of his reservations, Ray climbed aging wood steps onto the front porch that stretched the length of the log structure. He knocked lightly, not knowing for sure who or what would greet him. The door swung open, as if under its own power.

"Come in," Alice said. "I was expecting you."

The furnishings, arranged in a classical frontier motif, were sparse. In one corner stood a cast-iron, wood-burning stove. A bright blue porcelain coffee pot percolated, its bottom licked by flickering orange and blue flame. In another corner, a cowhide couch, black and white and brown, lounged in front of two towering pine wardrobes that he imagined were stocked with denim, sheepskin, and leather garments.

A ten-foot long dining table hewn out of pine split the room. Beyond the table, along the back wall, a stone fireplace framed a crackling fire that promised warmth and tranquility. On the front wall, centered between wood-frame windows, hung a glossy black-and-white photo of Roy Rogers straddling Trigger. The horse's hooves pawed the air as the iconic cowboy waved a comforting "Howdy."

The photo looked familiar to Ray. In fact, the entire cabin prompted a sense of déjà vu. A second later, it hit him. The house reminded him of a bunkhouse he had known as a child. For three consecutive summers, starting when he was eleven, he had helped out on a dude ranch near the Black Mountains. The head wrangler—a family friend who agreed to give him a crash course as a ranch-hand—had decorated his cabin in a similar fashion: homey, bare bones, practical. Buck was his name—he was a tough-as-nails cowpoke and a lonesome stoic whose weathered skin and watery eyes told a tale of hard work and heartbreak. Ray, who had admired the old cowboy, had even tried to emulate his slow-gaited walk and Southwestern drawl.

Remembering that he was in the presence of Alice, he blushed—even as a child he had been a shameless romantic. He looked up to see if she had noticed. She merely gestured for him to sit at the table.

"It's nice in here," he said.

"What did you expect?"

"I wasn't expecting anything. I followed you. Here I am." He studied the one-room cabin. "What are we doing here?"

"You wanted to learn about the spirit."

"Not exactly. You claimed I wasn't spiritual. Then, in the middle of our little spat, you skipped out."

"Spat?" A wry smile crossed her lips. "I'm not here to argue with you."

"No, of course not," he replied with sarcasm. "You were

sitting peacefully at the base of the tree. I came by and…" He fumbled to find the right words.

"You were faced with a dilemma. If you're not a spirit, how could you be spiritual?" she interjected. "Some people talk about being spiritual. But they really believe they're nothing but a body. I suppose they mean they're compassionate or they 'feel the energy' or they experience altruistic thoughts."

"Just because the meaning of a word evolves, doesn't mean we have to discard it. After they discovered there was no soul—"

"Discovered there was no soul? Hardly. They quit looking." She studied him. "I don't want to argue. Maybe it's best you go on your way."

Stunned, Ray looked for a smile or a twinkle in her brilliant blue eyes, anything to suggest she was kidding. Seeing the gravity of her expression, he fumbled. Where was he supposed to go? Yes, there was something he was supposed to do, if he could only remember…

"Well, if you're not leaving," she said, assuming a professorial demeanor, "it's time for a history lesson. In the late 1800s, psychologists experienced dreadful feelings of inferiority. The physical sciences were experiencing breakthrough after breakthrough. Psychologists desperately desired the esteem that physicists enjoyed. So, they assumed, it made sense for them to abandon the study of man's spirit. There were just too many complications when it came to the soul. They turned their focus to animal physiology: chickens, dogs, and rats. Had they suddenly discovered that man lacked a soul? No, they simply tossed the idea out the window."

"That's not exactly the story," Ray said, recalling his studies. A decade ago, he had experienced a period of unsettling doubt. At that time, he knew that if he hoped to make sense of the world, he would need a deeper well of wisdom from which to draw insights. He had enrolled at the university and leaped headfirst into the study of philosophy. As a result, he now had enough knowledge to know that Alice was preaching nonsense.

"Thanks to science, we understand that we humans evolved from a simple organism," he said. "The mystery of how we think and feel, all of our psychology, is locked up in the story of that evolution." Ignoring her look of disdain, he continued, "Evolutionary psychologists and cultural biologists have tracked our emotions, our beliefs, and our customs back to our earliest origins. How we think and feel and everything we believe is the product of years of evolution—"

"Evolution?" She snickered as she adjusted the flame under the coffee pot. She mocked him, "Oh, I see. But what evolves? Oh, the *body* evolves. But we were not talking about the body, we were talking about the soul."

Ray felt the sting of her sarcasm but he wasn't about to concede. "Our brains are highly evolved, more so than those of other creatures. That's why we reason and why we feel complex emotions. Why we believe we're special. It's why we dream up spirits and gods. It's why we create myths. Religion was an evolutionary adaptation that encouraged us to be nice to one another, so we would not kill off our species. And that's not a bad adaptation."

She eyed him with a smirk.

"This is well-researched science."

"Are you sure?" she asked. "Are you very, very sure?"

Ray flinched. The sarcasm, the barbed tone, the playful smile, and the mocking tilt of her eyebrows—it all reminded him of someone. His mind drifted back to high school, to Alexandra, to the first time he had fallen for a girl. It was also, he recalled, the first time he had been shot down by a girl.

Back in high school he had tried to play it cool. No grand gestures. No embarrassing confessions of love. A few half-hearted passes were all he could muster. It wasn't good enough. Alex seemed to float in a higher sphere of existence. Armed with a razor-sharp wit, she whittled "uncool" classmates into human kindling. Ray quickly found out what it meant to be on the receiving end of her verbal knife.

Even back then, he had realized that storming such a person's defenses would be an invitation to a perpetual dual, a never-ending verbal battle he could never win. He wondered if Alice was another Alex, barricaded behind an ego fortified with barbed wire. Could he break through to uncover a more genuine self? It was a risk he decided to take.

"Our consciousness emerges from the integrated neural activity of the brain," he said. "The 'I' is an illusion. It doesn't exist. The brain creates a mental model—"

Alice smirked with unmasked disdain.

"Ah, I see. I'm not ready for the path," he said.

Her stern glance sent a warning. He was on the verge of being booted from the cabin and set adrift in the wilderness.

"Not ready at all." She gawked for emphasis—shades of Alexandra.

Ray tensed. He felt like an awkward teenager trying not to humiliate himself in front of his classmates and here was Alice, talking to him as if he were the classroom dunce. *You're a grown man, he told himself. These girlish antics should not bother you. Laugh it off.*

"We're talking about a soul," she went on. "Not a body. But if you must bring up the Theory of Evolution, let me correct your misgivings. It's conjecture. Incomplete. Exact history is unknown. And the record possesses huge gaping holes. They simply packaged conjecture."

"So there's nothing to it?"

"Bio-organisms interact with their environment and change as a result. Elementary."

Of course, it's child's play.

"Forms change. How and why is not fully understood. Instead, we have speculation."

Ray took a moment to prepare his rebuttal. She might seem emotionally immature, but her intellect could not be laughed off.

"You're a Creationist?" he queried. "Or maybe you're pushing Intelligent Design? You're talking about God, aren't you? This is about the Big Watchmaker in the Sky, isn't it?"

He recalled the ideas of the nineteenth-century Anglican clergyman William Paley. In *Natural Theology*, Paley argued that if someone walking across the heath stumbled upon a stone, they could reasonably assume the stone was a product of nature. But, if they stumbled upon a watch, they would be forced to conclude it had been designed. Watch components were clearly assembled to accomplish a purpose that went beyond the function of any single one of its parts. A watch was meant to keep time, and yet none of its components—gears, springs, chains, and the like—were created with time-keeping in mind. Therefore, someone must have designed the watch and assembled the pieces for such a purpose.

Ray was surprised that his memory remained clear when it came to Intelligent Design. He recalled how ID proponents cleaned up Paley's argument and introduced an argument for "irreducible complexity" in biological systems. Like a watch, some biological systems must have been assembled with an overall function in mind. Irreducibly complex biological systems could not be reduced to random mutation—they had to be assembled with an overall purpose in mind. ID proponents used an analogy: if all the parts of a watch were scattered about out in a field, they would never spontaneously form a watch. Instead, there must be an Intelligent Designer and God was the primary candidate.

Alice giggled, then spoke up, "We do not have to talk about God. Not yet. Consider bio-engineers who modify genetic properties of plants and animals. What are they, if not intelligent designers?"

"Well…" Ray stumbled. He was dealing with someone who could argue at his level. He would have to shift his strategy.

But before he could mount an attack she continued. "A bio-engineer is an intelligent being who designs and modifies bio-organisms. That's an empirical example that proves intelligent design is real. It plays a role."

"But they're scientists. People like us."

"They're still intelligent designers."

Ray battled growing regret. If they kept arguing at this rate, they'd be stuck in this cabin until next winter. It was his fault. He had followed her down the rabbit hole when he should have simply changed the topic. He should have walked away and minded his own business.

He looked out the window. A storm was gathering. He needed a retreat strategy. As he tried to remember the path that led back to the trailhead, vertigo flooded his mind once again. A faint memory flashed—he had been driving on an icy and winding mountain road. Had that been earlier in the day or many weeks ago? He wished his mind would quit playing tricks on him.

He tried to swallow the panic, but it rushed upon him in waves, drowning his mind. A strategy. He needed a strategy. Perhaps he could call for help. Chase could pick him up, or she would call one of his hiking buddies for help. Reaching into his jacket pocket, he searched for his phone. His fingers brushed up against lint, but nothing else. He patted the pockets of his jeans and found nothing. He ran his eyes over the floor of the cabin. Nothing. His phone was gone. He was stranded.

He looked up to find Alice looking at him with an empty expression. Ray felt as if he were naked, as if she had exposed his vulnerability. Fear gave way to anger. He wanted to run as far away as he could from that placid expression. As if in response to his mood, the room grew darker. A specter of extreme loneliness crept up over him.

Worries danced in his mind: *What if Alice ran away a second time? What if he was stranded without a companion?*

He had been in worse situations before. He was an experienced hiker. Everything would turn out—as long as he kept his head. Unfortunately, the more he tried to comfort himself, the harder it became to control the looming panic.

For some reason, he needed Alice. He wasn't sure why, but he sensed that when she left, all hope would be lost. The thought sparked renewed determination—he would hang on. No matter how unpleasant, he had to keep talking. He had to keep Alice happy. And that meant he had to finish the debate.

6

Lani was well into her second shift. Her brain was on cruise control and her metabolism rested in energy-saver mode. Not quite relaxed, neither was she fully alert. The weakened defensive perimeter of her mind allowed stray thoughts to intrude and her imagination danced with strangers.

This evening her gaze wandered to ICU 7 where Ray remained in a coma. His business partner and close friend, Hal, was on watch. Moonlight through the window softly silhouetted his sturdy frame, casting glints of bluish light off his sandy hair. Randi, the patient's mother was also present.

Lani had taken to watching over Randi with the attentiveness of a den mother. She tried to find a hint of surrender in Randi's demeanor, but failed. Though Randi's face was painted with grief, it was also chiseled with a warrior's determination.

As she watched their vigil, she was overtaken by weariness and soon succumbed to the early morning daze that cursed the graveyard shift. She was transported into imagery that so often put in an appearance in the dead of the night. She imagined a bridge shrouded in fog and on that bridge ICU visitors became ghostly figures milling about in slow motion, waiting for loved ones to return from the "other side."

It was a fantasy that had haunted her hundreds of times as she had struggled to stay awake at her post. On occasion she felt her entire life was lived in such a state of limbo, in an imaginary land between this world and the next. More and more often, her mind was held hostage to the drama on the bridge. When weariness lowered her defenses, the ghosts haunting the bridge gained access to her inner world and lured her into joining the vigil on the bridge. When that happened, she visualized patients, those who had visited death's doorstep, making their way through the fog and back into the arms of relatives and friends. But there were times when no one reappeared. There were nights when the bridge remained empty, abandoned. When that happened, she was a witness as loved ones with broken hearts made grim exits.

Lani had tried to corral the emotions that came with her ICU assignment. She had tried to divide her life into emotional silos: she sought to separate her vocation from her civilian life as a mother, sister, daughter and friend. Some days it worked. But there had been times when she was tending to mundane chores, like shopping or visiting friends, that the defensive shield had fallen and she had been overwhelmed by the fragility of life. In those moments, she wished she had chosen a different profession.

Doctors had it figured out, she mused. They were in and out of a patient's life before they glimpsed the bridge. They knew how to avert their gaze. They remained tethered to solid ground, tasked with anchoring patients to life. They could not allow themselves to be lured onto the bridge where outcomes were in doubt. Thus, doctors knew little about death. They preferred it that way. They played on life's team.

Emerging from her reverie, she glanced once again toward ICU 7 and checked on Ray. Though he was in critical condition, it was still too early to predict the outcome. She had seen comatose patients awaken and make full recoveries. Then again other patients in even better condition had taken a sudden turn for the worse. *Either way, this drama was not yet ready to end.*

7

Alice met Ray's gaze. The radiance of her blue eyes unnerved him. Something in her look put him on edge. *Was it pity? Mourning?* No, perhaps it was compassion. There was something timeless—something that touched eternity—in the sadness of her expression. He nearly succumbed to an odd urge to weep, but then he recovered his emotional equilibrium and centered himself firmly in his intellect.

"I'll be okay," he said.

"So you made a mistake," she said. "Mistakes can be corrected."

"And my mistake was…"

"You assumed consciousness emerges from the brain. You assumed conscious feelings, thoughts, and beliefs originate in the brain." She studied him as if he were a student who had unexpectedly flunked the final. "You believe consciousness emerges from structure. And yet the correct answer is the opposite: consciousness gives rise to structure. All forms emerge from consciousness."

"But—"

"No 'buts.' If you explore consciousness, you'll find a huge gap between brain activity and conscious experience—"

"Maybe the work is incomplete."

"Incomplete?" Her smirk taunted. "In spite of decades of conjecture, there's no proof that brain activity is equivalent to consciousness. The gap between the brain and consciousness that they call the 'hard problem' remains as daunting as ever. There's a reason they'll never close that gap. You know what it is?"

He didn't know, but he wasn't about to concede his ignorance. He chose silence. The drip of the percolating coffee marked the passing time.

"You mean dualism," he speculated at last. "Body *and* spirit. But that idea has been discredited."

She raised a skeptical eyebrow.

"Descartes," he said, referring to the philosopher who had struggled with the question of the conscious observer. "He toyed with the idea of the theater of the mind. He wanted to know who viewed the moment-to-moment stream of consciousness. He was mocked for saying there was a little man inside—"

"Of course there is no little man. Descartes did not say that," she replied. "A soul is not a little man sitting inside a head. A spirit is not a thing. It's immaterial. Consciousness is immaterial."

"The sum of brain activity—"

"Nope. That does not hold up."

"But duality is not—"

"Your friends, the skeptics, put forth a false picture of

dualism, a straw-man argument. The only thing they knocked down was the silly straw man they created. The only thing they discredited was their own idea."

"And the reality is—"

"The body is a stimulus-response bio-organism, a bio-robot. In contrast, the conscious you is a soul. When spirit joins body, the result is a wonderful composite, a human."

She poured two cups of coffee slowly and deliberately, giving him time to think, time to reconsider his decision to stay.

Lighten up, he warned himself. "Look, if you want, we can change the subject," he said, offering a truce.

"That wouldn't make any sense," she replied. "These are the questions on your mind. We must clear up any confusion."

"I suppose we don't have to."

He could tell her patience was wearing thin. She replied, "Yes, but we must. You don't understand, do you?"

No, he did not understand. There was a great deal about this evening he did not understand. And yet he felt he needed to keep going—the next verbal volley might shed light on the awful mystery he had not resolved.

"You used to love to debate. At… the… university," she said. "You wrestled with philosophy. "Your mentor was Professor—"

"Professor Kinder was my thesis adviser, for a while," Ray acknowledged. She had hit him with a surprise out of left field. Was she playing parlor tricks?

He tried a change of tactic to help him regain the upper

hand. "Why don't we use our time wisely and get to know each other? Maybe we could become friends. Is this your home?"

"Home away from home," she said. "You will come to know me soon enough. First, let's get to know you. You've become confused by what you've learned about life."

"I should be getting home." He covered his frustration with a polite smile. He would not enjoy stumbling down the mountain in the dark, but he felt the need to escape. *There was somewhere he was supposed to be.*

"How far do you think you'll get?" Alice nodded toward the window.

Ray stole a glance: the gloomy weather had not improved. The thick fog that obscured the trees had not lifted. A fireplace log crackled, extending an invitation for him to stay and soak up its warmth. The photo of Roy Rogers perched on Trigger bathed him with a glow of fond memories.

Alice's voice, softer than before, pulled him back into the conversation. "Make yourself comfortable. Let's clear up a few things."

He flopped down on the cowhide couch and puzzled over his companion. Why was she so interested? And why was she so darn serious? Was she a former student he had supervised? Did she hold a grudge over a bad grade?

He said, "Go on."

"Scientists assume that only the material world exists. They overlook a model that incorporates material and immaterial elements. The false assumptions of materialism have doomed science to failure."

Ray would not allow her to have the last word. "They realize that consciousness, like computer software, is a process—"

"A machine such as a computer performs only mechanical computation. It is incapable of conscious thought. You can appreciate the difference, can't you?"

"A robot cannot become conscious?"

"Exactly. True artificial intelligence is a fantasy."

"But if there's enough complexity—"

"Complexity has nothing to do with it. That's an argument used to disguise the gap between mechanics and consciousness. A black box solution."

"Black box?"

"When something happens that we do not understand, when something happens that we cannot observe, we call our guess a 'black box' solution. People who equate brain activity with consciousness make such a black box argument. They have no evidence so they simply assume 'facts' they cannot observe—"

"They deduce answers," he interrupted.

"Guesses. Conjecture. Hunches."

"Models that tell us our bodies and our brains are complex machines," he retorted.

Alice pulled an aging water-damaged cardboard shoebox out of a cupboard and dumped its contents: matchbox cars, plastic robots, a cat's eye marble, and a "Slinky." The toys, similar to Ray's childhood possessions, triggered nostalgia.

"Our bodies *are* machines," she continued. "But any machine, even a bio-machine, is never truly conscious. It

operates on a stimulus-response basis, but that's not consciousness."

Ray scooped up a miniature robot and marched it from knot to knot on the pine table, manipulating its tiny plastic legs. "A computer or robot has memory—"

"It records data but such a recording is not consciousness," she said. "Storing or manipulating records is mechanical. A machine can store, manipulate, and compute—but that's not consciousness."

She retrieved a rock from the fireplace mantel. "A piece of matter, like this rock, can exist for a billion years and never become conscious. Consciousness is not a property of matter. You can configure matter any way you want and it will never become conscious. Only the spirit is conscious."

"We cannot know spirit. We cannot know that which we can't see," he said.

"You suffer from blind materialism," she snorted, exasper-ated.

Ray took one more look out the window. At the very least, he would have to wait until morning.

"Prove it," he said, trying to hold back his bitterness. "Prove that consciousness even exists."

"This is going to be more difficult than I imagined. But I'll not turn you out, yet. Give me a minute to consider my words."

Grateful for the respite, Ray waited for her to collect her thoughts.

"How about a quiz?" she asked. "What is more real than that which you observe?"

He shrugged.

"The observer. The observer is more real than that which it observes. The observer is primary," she added.

"Run that past me again," he said, not certain he followed her logic.

"Materialism takes into account only 'things observed.' Materialists forget the observer. They fail to acknowledge the observer is the basis of all reality. The act of observing—what we call consciousness—is basic to all reality."

Classic chicken-and-egg argument, Ray mused. The act of observing, the state of being conscious, involved both an observer and something to observe. Which was primary? Could you have one without the other?

She continued. "The observer, the conscious being, is aware of being aware. It can exist without anything to observe. It can simply be aware of being aware."

"What does that even mean?" he asked.

"It means pure awareness or pure consciousness exists. One does not need something to observe. Consider the mystics who meditate and seek a state of unattached awareness. Their goal is to achieve a state of simply being-aware-of-being-aware. They've learned that the most basic component of reality is consciousness."

"But—"

"Without the observer, nothing is ever observed. We cannot know if anything exists separate from our consciousness."

"And yet science—"

"Scientists base their knowledge on observation. But they

do not understand the observer so the entire house of cards collapses."

"If that is true—"

"If one does not understand the observer, the cornerstone of all science is an unknown. Materialistic science rests on an unknown; it is built on a foundation of sand."

Her sharp eyes, full of curiosity, studied him. "You still believe you're only a body?"

"Yeah, I suppose."

She eyed him with mild concern that deepened into grave concern as she gazed out the window into the dark.

"What is it?" Ray asked. He was tired of her inscrutable moods. "What's wrong?"

"Are you afraid?" she asked.

"Should I be?"

She answered with a pained look that she did her best to soften with a tight smile.

I'll take that as yes, he thought. He then wondered, *how will I ever get out of this mess?*

8

Chase and Hal Sutherland, standing on opposite sides of the bed, studied Ray's lifeless body. Chase, sensing Hal was having a difficult time, placed a reassuring hand on his forearm.

She was correct. Hal, tall at six-foot-four, did feel out of place: he belonged in the woods, camping, felling trees, repelling off granite cliffs. Hospitals were too far removed from nature's steady pulse for his woodsy tastes.

Chase had found it easy to read Hal ever since he first became Ray's partner in a new business venture, a start-up called Changes in Action, a company that had stalled on the financial runway, leaving them waiting for elusive funding that had never arrived. She watched as Hal struggled to find the words to express his troubled emotions. She offered a sympathetic smile that invited him to unburden.

"The investors finally gave us the green light," he said. His voice was devoid of the enthusiasm that should have accompanied the good news. "After all these months, the damn committee finally approved our proposal. Ray was on his way into town to bring you the good news. He didn't want to phone. He wanted to see your face when he told you."

That made two important messages that had gone undelivered, Chase noted with bitterness. When she had discovered she was pregnant, she had debated whether to tell Ray, given the tenuous status of the fledgling business venture. For days she had vacillated. She had plenty of time, she had told herself. She now regretted those lost days. If he had made it home that evening they would now be celebrating.

Why had Fate knocked Ray out of the game the moment their lives were about to change for the better? Ray had spent years planning Changes in Action, a program with an Outward Bound style. They planned to recruit teachers from inner-city schools and transport them to the wilderness for old-fashioned survival training. Ray and Hal would coach them through the transformative experience.

As Ray explained the idea, the program's goal had little to do with wilderness survival skills; rather, it was intended to immerse teachers in situations whose success depended on teamwork. The training would serve as a catalyst for collaboration. Ray believed students should learn to compete, but also learn to collaborate.

Hal exhaled, as if he was spitting out a curse or expelling a foul-tasting poison. "I'm not going forward without him. This was his dream. And this—"

"Hal, we can't be certain he's going to make it."

"I know. They've done all they can. Now it's up to—it's up to someone. If it's up to Ray, he'll pull through. He's not a quitter."

Randi entered. Though Chase had introduced Hal earlier, they had hardly spoken. After an awkward moment, Randi broke the ice, "My son admired you and called you, 'An amazing force of nature.' Said he would climb any peak, as long as you were in the lead."

"Ray led as much as he followed. There wasn't a challenge that could beat him."

Randi sensed the doubt in Hal's voice; his optimism was more wishful thinking than prophecy. Nevertheless, Randi appreciated his sentiment and nearly melted when he wrapped her in a hug. His generous strength gave her balance.

They were interrupted by Dr. Seidman's entrance.

"All blood relatives I assume," he challenged.

"I'm the mother," Randi said.

Seidman glanced at Hal and Chase, who remained silent. His meaning was clear: *you're dismissed.* Apparently he wanted to conduct "family only" business.

Hal bristled. More than one bar brawl had been the result of some unlucky soul treating him with disrespect. His philosophy of life was strictly egalitarian: all men deserved respect, until they demonstrated otherwise.

Chase, sensing Hal's overheated emotions, broke the tension. "Good. We need a little time for personal business. Randi, can you handle whatever it is the doctor needs?"

Randi returned a weak nod. She did not relish facing off with another brusque doctor. Dr. Seidman pulled up a chair and gestured for her to sit opposite him. She obeyed.

"Dr. Seidman," he said, extending his hand.

"Dr. Sloane's associate?"

"No. Psychologist. I work with families. I help them explore strategies for coping with hardship. The hospital considers me an important member of the team in circumstances like these."

"Circumstances?"

Dr. Seidman studied Randi, silently appraising and evaluating.

At first, Randi fidgeted, but then realized that she, too, could engage in her own evaluation. She cast a critical eye on Seidman. He was distant and overly professional, and though he dressed neatly, his appearance lacked any personal charm. He looked, she noted with wry disapproval, as if his mother had dressed him. Even more unsettling was her impression that the psychologist lacked emotional strings she could pull.

"Questions?" he asked. "Or anything you would like to share regarding your son?"

The man was fishing, *but for what?* Remaining noncommittal, she said, "I want Ray to get better. Is there something the doctors want you to tell me?"

"I'm sorry. I didn't mean to cause alarm. There's nothing new to report, good or bad. I'm simply extending an invitation. If you should ever want to discuss anything, I'm here. We're both human so we realize how difficult it can be to come to grips with uncertainty."

Randi slipped into her thoughts, unaware that she was speaking aloud... "Always figured I would be the one hooked up to a machine, that I would be the one to make the awkward exit. I thought Ray would have to deal with my passing."

"Life hands us surprises," the psychologist said. "It would be nice if everything went according to our wishes. It would be wonderful if we could stick to our own script. But we live in a universe of probability. Every day we roll the dice. We can never be certain what fate holds in store."

"Fate?"

Seidman gazed at Ray's bandaged body. And then, after noticing that Randi was growing increasingly tense, he made an offer, "You must be famished. There's a cafeteria downstairs. Care to join me?"

"I would be delighted," she replied, even though she wasn't hungry and she hated to leave Ray alone, in the remote chance he should wake while she was gone. Nonetheless, she grabbed her purse and followed, relieved at the chance to have a change of scenery.

In the elevator, Seidman, his eyes locked on the floor indicator, continued his counseling, "I know it's difficult to think we're just a part of nature's grand scheme. Yet, if we stop to think about it, we should consider our existence improbable luck for which we can be grateful."

Randi studied his reflection in the elevator door. Was he trying to comfort her or trying to convey a metaphysical lesson?

"I suppose I *am* grateful," she said after a brief pause. "One might even consider our existence a miracle."

"A miracle? Perhaps the real reason is less glamorous; maybe we're the result of a grand cosmic accident."

As Randi stepped out of the elevator she responded with a touch of sarcasm, "It has occurred to me there might be a bit more to the story."

9

"Time to sleep on it," Alice said, snuggling up on the cow-hide-upholstered couch in the corner. Within minutes, she drifted off.

Ray assumed her arsenal of one-liners had been depleted. He was being given a welcome respite. Feeling a damp chill seep into the cabin, he squatted in front of the fire. As he watched the flames dance, he spotted a steamer trunk nestled in a nook. He crossed and popped its dust-covered latch. Inside, he found a cache of old books, toys and trinkets. These were similar to the matchbox cars and miniature robots Alice displayed previously. Childhood memories flooded his mind.

Alice, too, was a memory. Not the girl napping on the couch—she was still a mystery to him—but the Alice she resembled, the Alice who wandered through the wonderland of Lewis Carroll's imagination.

An ironic smile crossed Ray's lips. He had always been a pragmatist, a skeptic with a penchant for overthinking everything. Yet here he was, lost in his own wonderland. He glanced at the sleeping girl. They had started on the wrong foot. With a twinge of remorse, he realized he had been rude when he had nicknamed her "Alice." As soon as she awoke, he would apologize and ask her name. He would change his tone. Though she clearly could handle the hard-edged dialect of scientific debate, perhaps she preferred the colorful language of metaphor.

Shortly after he had made the decision to remedy his treatment of Alice and make up the damage, his thoughts wandered to his former thesis adviser, Dr. Alan Kidner, a noted lecturer in epistemology, the study of "how we know." Alice had dredged up his past with the professor—how she had done so remained a troubling mystery. However, so many mysteries were popping up that it made no sense to dwell on this one.

Kidner's philosophical arguments, which were now old memories, danced in Ray's memory. His professor lectured that when it came to human knowledge, significant gaps remained, especially in the field of consciousness studies. He had expressed a desire to close those gaps. Understanding consciousness was not only the professor's Holy Grail, it was also a Damocles' sword hanging over his head. He feared that if he did not solve the riddle his work was destined for the dustbin.

Early on Kidner had seemed a perfect mentor. Unfortunately, the professor had become increasingly isolated from his colleagues. He had spent too much time grumbling that no new ground was being broken in philosophy, especially at the university. Though Ray had admired Kidner's passion, he had also worried that he had hitched his future to a fading star. He had feared being condemned to an academic Siberia, relegated to a life as a social and intellectual outcast.

Ray allowed the memories to flow and recalled snippets of one lecture: "Consciousness is the sole portal through which all knowledge flows. Consciousness is *the* primary constant in the universe. Abandon consciousness and you abandon all knowledge," the philosopher had lectured. "Our consciousness figures into all our equations and yet it remains an unknown, which means all science is incomplete."

Ray knew these ideas were not foreign to Alice. He glanced at her but she was still napping. Guilt arose, without being summoned. The compassion she had shown him was a haunting reminder—he had failed to show his professor the kindness that he had deserved. This prompted Ray to recall a disastrous dinner party held at the professor's house.

That evening a handful of undergraduates and one graduate student from "the other camp," a young lady named Hilary, had assembled for food and conversation. Vegetables—squash, peppers, potatoes and onions—had been skewered and browned on the grill. Homemade bread was served fresh out of the oven. In addition, an assortment of pastas—tortellini, angel hair, and gnocchi's—had graced the dinner table. Bottles of Cabernet Sauvignon, Merlot, and Chianti had been uncorked.

The safety lines that ordinarily tethered inquiring student minds had been cut that evening, freeing young imaginations to soar to rarefied Platonic altitudes. Ray was unable to pinpoint exactly when the evening took a dark turn. In retrospect, he suspected it had been when Hilary first challenged the professor. He vaguely recalled her words, "Dualism, the antiquated idea that there's a body *and* a soul, is an artifact that has gone the way of the witch doctor. No longer in fashion."

"So philosophy has become a matter of fashion?" Kidner had lowered his fork and leaned his elbows on the table, prepared for a battle of wits. He had glanced at Ray, apparently expecting his student to take up his defense. Ray, however, was embarrassed at being singled out. He had frozen. Instead of speaking up, he had looked down at his plate and twirled his pasta.

Kidner had cleared his throat and continued: "In *The Republic* Plato concludes with the tale of a soldier who dies on the battlefield, and then, days later, comes back to life with a detailed story of the Other Side, having undergone what we now call a near-death experience."

Ray recalled the professor had risen and crossed to the fireplace where he had lit a cigar that had filled the room with fragrant clouds of smoke. An undergraduate had wrinkled her nose, filing a silent objection. Her dinner companion, in a defiant response, had solicited a cigar from the professor and had lit up as well.

"A few things have changed since the days of Plato," Hilary had countered with a trace of a sneer.

"Have they? Near-death experiences are as common today as when Plato related his tale. These reports amaze us, just as in ancient times. In Plato's time, they shared accounts of mystical experiences. Thousands of years later, we do the same. Things haven't changed."

"What has changed is science," Ray had interjected. "We've shown these experiences are products of brain chemistry. Imagination. Hallucination."

"Ah, but have we?" the professor had countered.

Ray had glanced up in time to see the hurt in his mentor's eyes. Looking back all these years later, his betrayal still elicited guilt.

At the time, Ray had not given enough thought to his improvised alliance with Hilary. In retrospect, he realized he had been seduced by her charm, rather than convinced by her arguments. At the time he had justified his treason. He had convinced himself that a tag team of lightweight grad students made for a fair fight with an academic heavyweight. But Kidner's expression had revealed unexpected vulnerability. The department had abandoned him, and then Ray had also jumped ship.

"I'm not a neuroscientist, I'm a philosopher," the professor had continued. "However, as philosophers, it is our duty to keep the scientists honest. In that task, we've failed. We have conformed, so as to be 'fashionable.' We no longer lead with courage. We've become a pack of cowards following fads."

Dr. Kidner had waved his cigar like an improvised lecture pointer. "No one has demonstrated NDE's are simply imagination. Many espouse that assumption, in their attempt to bolster a weak theory. But they fail to provide evidence or even a decent argument. All the evidence shows the brain-chemistry model fails to explain the NDE."

Hilary had tried to interrupt, but Kidner had cut her off. "The most important evidence comes from those who report seeing their own body from a position *outside* the body. Remarkable, isn't it?"

Though Ray had heard talk of such accounts, he had never considered that they might be real. He had barely given the claims a second thought.

"There are reports of people looking down on doctors in the operating room," the professor continued. "They have viewed grieving relatives while floating outside their body. As far as I know, their brains did not pop out of their skulls and float up to the ceiling. Therefore, the reasonably intelligent person, after carefully studying the reports, must conclude that such experiences are not the result of brain chemistry run amuck." He had flicked the ash from his cigar into the fireplace with a flourish.

"But floating outside the body must be make-believe, right?" Ray had asked. "An illusion?"

"Apparently not. Some accounts accurately describe events taking place while the body remains unconscious. They report perceptions taking place at a time when the brain is barely functioning. In some cases, people describe events that could be known *only* by viewing from a position outside their body."

"Cool," the undergraduate girl had blurted out, her fascination overruling her aversion to cigar smoke. With one salvo of slang she had replaced Ray as the professor's ally.

Her companion had smothered the smoldering ember at the tip of his cigar and had cleared his voice. "Uh, I had an experience like that. It wasn't during an operation. Nothing like that. I was with—" He had blushed, then had forged ahead. "With this girl." The dinner guests had responded with knowing chuckles.

"We were at a summer camp in the mountains. It was off-season. We found a vacant cabin and spent the night. For a couple hours, I fell into a deep slumber. When I woke I was 'standing' next to the bed, looking down on my body… and the girl next to me. It was weird. It wasn't a dream. I was awake. Like I am now."

"Creepy," his date had said with campfire-story awe. "What happened?"

"I thought to myself, let me see what I can do. Could I move around? Could I, you know, like, see things? I moved or floated toward the door and BAM—I slammed back into my body, hard. Like I had fallen from three feet above. My body jerked with the impact. That awakened… I didn't know what to say to her. Even now, I don't talk about it much. That's all."

After she had freshened the professor's goblet of Cabernet Sauvignon, Hilary argued, "That's not been replicated in the lab." Ray had wondered if red wine resembled hemlock. Socrates had defended his philosophy with his life. Would Kidner drink Hilary's less obvious poison, the venom in her argument?

"Dear, not all science takes place in the lab. Often we must go into the field to observe a phenomenon. At least until we understand enough to duplicate the conditions in the lab." His smile had turned ironic. "When the experiment involves putting subjects into near-death states, ethical questions must be considered."

Students had toasted a point well made. One young man had refilled their glasses.

Though the students had turned against Hilary, she had not surrendered. "So the argument that these experiences have not been replicated in the lab doesn't hold water?"

"It doesn't. It's merely an attempt to close the door on the subject before the real investigation even begins. Your objection is premature."

Ray had chimed in. "Those who claim they were outside—"

"Merely report what they experience," Kidner had fired back.

"But experience is not—"

"Not what? Near-death subjects perceive in the present, not in a dream state. Just like us, they know the difference between a dream and a waking moment. They've been awake before and they've had dreams before. They know the difference."

Damn, Ray had thought—how quickly he had made an enemy of someone he had respected.

"So why don't we listen to them?" Kidner had asked, rhetorically.

"Because they're lying?" Hilary had retorted.

"Ah, the skeptic's assumption. So, without investigation, we arbitrarily discount valid reports. A bit cynical."

He had been right, Ray mused. Skeptics dismissed reports before investigating. They were not alone. He was also pre-disposed to dismiss at first glance that which he found implausible. That was simply human nature.

"If we consider all subjective reports invalid and untrustworthy, we find ourselves on a very slippery slope," the professor had continued. "There is only one way we can collect raw data in our study of consciousness—we ask a subject what he experienced. This is obvious. If you discount subjective reports, you cannot study consciousness. You're finished."

He had then put another match to his cigar, signaling the conclusion of his argument. In retrospect, Ray realized Kidner had signaled the end of Ray's tenure as his student. Though Ray had initially thought his offense was minor, upon reflection it had dawned on him that he might be forced to secure another thesis advisor, *if* he could even find a professor willing to add him mid-semester. Ray had feared the prospect of losing Kidner's mentorship; but he had also felt powerless to change the course of events.

Now, as he studied Alice, he feared he was headed down that same disastrous path: his intransigence would alienate her, his skepticism would close doors, and in the end he would lose the friendship of someone who had shown him kindness.

10

Dr. Seidman navigated through a sea of nurses, doctors, and visitors. Randi struggled to keep up. As they rounded a corner and entered the cafeteria, Seidman broke his silence.

"You're religious?"

"Not particularly. Why?"

Dr. Seidman made straight for the buffet. After picking up a plate, he turned to Randi. "Religion makes sense. Belief is coded in our DNA. Our ancestors believed in the supernatural, and that allowed them to cope with threats to their survival."

"Go on," Randi encouraged.

"It was religious myths that prevented men from killing one another. The myths prevented our species from becoming extinct before we wandered out of the bush."

Randi became terribly aware of the smell of grease. Steaming pots of chicken, creamed corn … all looked unappetizing under the harsh fluorescent light.

"So religion is what keeps us from killing each other?" she asked. Refusing a plate, she followed Seidman through the line.

"Unfortunately, the supernatural myths no longer serve that purpose. The adaptation has lost its value. Religious beliefs that once supported survival now work against us. Those beliefs now motivate wars."

She may not have been an ardent believer, but she did not like the path his argument was taking. She knew that some conflicts had their origin in religious ideology, but those few cases were anomalies. Usually, desperate men used religion as a front to hide political goals. That was not real religion.

However, not wanting to incite an argument in the buffet line, she let the subject drop. Excusing herself, she selected a pre-packaged salad from a refrigerated display next to the cash register, paid the attendant in cash, and made her way into the main dining hall, an expansive room filled with cheap, brightly colored, mid-century décor.

Seidman claimed an empty table in the middle of the room, pulled out one of the plastic chairs, and sat at the rickety laminate table. Once Randi caught up, he continued his lecture.

"It's not all bad news. Myths may help us deal with death."

"How?"

"Belief in an afterlife allows us to go on with our lives, accepting the death of those we love. It creates a future for our loved ones, which allows us to go forward into *our* future. It's healthy."

"So a fantasy protects our emotions? But if I know the afterlife is mere fantasy, what good could it possibly do to pretend?" she asked.

"Intellectually, we know the fantasy is hardwired into our

genes. But that doesn't mean belief in an afterlife doesn't have value, from an emotional viewpoint. Of course, I'm not saying you must harbor such beliefs."

"You don't, do you?"

"I left that behind years ago."

"So when one dies, it's lights out," she said.

"What I believe is not important. What *is* important is that you have the emotional tools you need so you can deal with—"

"Deal with what? What are you getting at? You reject the afterlife on an intellectual basis. I got that. Now you want me to accept death as final so I will be relieved when my responsibility to Ray is over? Is that it?"

Randi's verbal jabs forced Seidman into a defensive posture. "Some people find comfort in knowing that once the body ceases to function… they become relieved the person no longer exists. They take emotional comfort in the finality. It provides closure. Sure, the abrupt transition is extremely upsetting but then they can move on, closing that chapter."

She crossed the line from conversation to confrontation. "So we're supposed to believe that life is an accident and death is equally arbitrary? We should take comfort in the belief that the universe began with a roll of the dice? We should be happy that life is simply a meaningless game?"

"I didn't say there was no meaning."

"No, you didn't. But that's the logical conclusion of your argument." She pushed her tray aside. "You mind answering a question?"

He nodded with a wary grimace.

"How does one hardwire religion into DNA? Where in those itsy-bitsy, tiny chemical strands are beliefs hidden? How are ideas bundled in the DNA and passed from generation to generation? Has anyone located an idea or a belief in a strand of DNA?"

"The term 'hardwired' is a metaphor." His answer was terse.

"A metaphor? Really? Look, I appreciate your attempt to help. I'm certain you're a valuable member of the hospital team. But, frankly, these theories are a little too far-fetched for my taste. Hardwiring religion into DNA?"

"I'm the one who should apologize," he said. "I didn't mean to veer off on a tangent. Whatever you believe, that's fine. I just want to help."

"Don't patronize me, okay? If we don't believe the same things—we'll have to work around that."

Randi placed her fork on the side of the plastic salad bowl: the lettuce was stale; the dressing was watery. She spotted Chase and Hal entering the dining room. She waved and they made their way to her table. Hal extended his hand to Seidman.

"Dr. Seidman, I'm sorry. When we were upstairs, I didn't recognize you," Hal said. "You're on the advisory committee for the Education Development Board, right?"

"Yes. Yes I am." Seidman said, pleasantly surprised that Hal recognized his status.

"I noticed your picture in the monthly newsletter. You

probably didn't recognize me either."

Seidman puzzled. Was there a reason he should recognize Hal?

"But maybe you recognized the patient in ICU 7, Ray Carte. The EDB approved funding for our program, Changes in Action. You must have approved our proposal."

"Now it's my turn to apologize," Seidman said, after a brief pause. "I didn't put it together. The Ray upstairs is the Ray Carte from Changes in Action?"

"As you can imagine, the project is now on hold."

"You helped my son with his funding?" Randi blurted out, barely suppressing her horrified surprise. "That was very kind."

She wished for a little pill that would make her disappear or for a time machine that would send her back to the moment just *before* she insulted the man responsible for funding her son's business.

"I didn't know your son personally. But I was impressed with his proposal, as were the other board members." He noticed her embarrassment. "Don't worry, he wasn't planning to do any work that involved hardwiring."

"Well, at least we can be thankful for that," she said. She was glad Ray had not been there to watch her insult his funding source. It was the kind of thing that gave mothers a bad reputation.

Chase threw Randi a lifeline. "We're heading upstairs. Would you like to come with us?"

"Yes, it's time. Thank you, Dr. Seidman, for dining with

me. I appreciate your kindness."

Still mortified, Randi floated out of the cafeteria close behind Chase and Hal. Of all the psychologists in the world, why had Seidman been assigned to Ray's case? She found herself wondering how he now felt about Ray's proposal. Had she tainted Ray's prospects? Had she thrown mud into the pool of goodwill? Unnerved, she recalled the barbs she had launched at the psychologist.

Perhaps he was right. Perhaps life *was* a never-ending game of chance, one big high-stakes game on the Vegas strip. In real life, she realized, players could not walk away and cut their losses. Once the game started, the dice kept on rolling no matter how deep in the hole a player found himself. Not much of a game, she concluded.

Randi took a deep breath as she entered Ray's hospital room. She knew that, if the dice did not soon land in her favor, she faced some tough decisions.

11

Ray glanced at Alice, asleep on the couch. Seeing that she was outside the fire's circle of warmth, he rummaged through one of the oak wardrobes and retrieved a wool blanket, which he gently laid over her. It was a simple act of kindness, which reminded him of earlier missed opportunities. Life presented ample opportunity for demonstrations of kindness, he mused, whether or not he heeded the call was another matter.

As he scanned his failing, a barrage of memories assaulted him with guilt. One memory in particular nagged at him: he recalled the morning that followed the professor's dinner party. Ray had paid a visit to the philosophy department, hoping to smooth over any upset that lingered. He had been prepared to proffer an apology: he had planned to joke with the professor and blame his lapse on the fine wine. However, his plan had backfired.

As he had approached the office he had found the door open; his professor had been working at his decades-old computer. Though Ray had knocked, Kidner had kept his back to the door. In retrospect, he knew he should have seen the behavior for what it was—the aloof demeanor of an absent-minded professor. He should have checked his ego. However, at that time, in an instant, his good intentions had faded. Perhaps his guilt had made him ready for battle.

"You know, Professor, some academic researchers disagree with you."

"Who might that be?" Kidner had replied without turning around.

"Scientists who studied the objective facts. Scientists who study neurons and synapses and neurochemicals—rather than subjective reports."

"You fail to see the paradox," the professor had responded with a weary sigh.

"Let me guess. The only way any scientist can know anything is through his or her own subjective awareness?"

"Exactly. When they claim subjective experience cannot be trusted, they destroy their own argument—because every single one of their claims is based on subjective observation. They negate their own argument. Silly if you ask me."

Kidner had spun around to study his collection of pipes without looking at Ray. His Jack Terrier, Sherpa, had awakened from his nap and sneezed.

"No doubt that's Sherpa's editorial comment on my smoking habits," the professor had joked.

Sherpa had studied Ray with a skeptical and slightly hostile tilt of his tiny head.

The professor had smiled sarcastically at the dog's posture. "He's wondering if you got laid last night."

"It made no sense for the lamb to lie down with the lioness."

"Wise decision."

You're the one that invited her, Ray thought. *You must've known what would happen.*

Ray had resented the professor's disdain and he had allowed that irritation to further poison the conversation. Ray, in retrospect, knew the professor had been right. Ray had slipped: rather than defend his mentor's work, he had tried to impress the girl.

Looking back, Ray realized the professor had been justified in his resentment toward the academic community. Years of attacks had destroyed any patience he once had. Ray should have perceived the man's vulnerability. Ray should have recognized the underlying emotional pain, which had driven the professor to argue his views with uncommon fervor.

The professor had told Ray, "These scientists you admire pretend to be objective. Their charade is amusing or perhaps simply cunning."

"Scientists undergo peer review to make sure their work is objective," Ray had retorted.

"Ah, but what is peer review? One subjective observer huddles with another subjective observer. They agree on subjective observations. They form a subjective consensus. That's all. Think about it. If you add one subjective observation to another subjective observation, the result is simply subjective agreement."

Kidner had hoisted the tiny sentry Sherpa off the floor and had held him in his lap. The dog had pointed his whiskered snout at Ray, had fixed his stare on him. He had recognized Ray was his master's Judas. That morning, Ray had wondered what Sherpa would be like drunk—a good-natured party animal or vicious beast? While staring at the terrier, Ray had silently pondered the professor's ideas.

However, unfortunately, the professor had misread Ray's silence and had assumed Ray was being contrary. This had provoked him to continue slamming home his point: "When two or three or a thousand individuals agree, we have inter-subjective agreement. When you add more and more subjective observers you do not transcend the subjective. Simple addition is not magic that delivers us from the realm of subjective observation."

Kidner had rubbed the Sherpa's ears; the dog had licked his master's beard. That morning, they had been an impressive duo. Ray recalled how his combative stance had softened.

"If we remove all subjective awareness from the world, does the proverbial 'tree in the forest' still exist?" The professor had paused for effect. "Of course, we can't know, can we?"

That was true, Ray had been forced to admit. There was no way to know if an objective world exists independent of all subjective awareness. If you removed all conscious beings from the world, there would be no way to know anything. For the first time, Ray had grasped the fatal glitch in the science-is-objective mantra.

Ray thought back to how the Professor had lowered Sherpa gently to the floor, had shuffled over to a blackboard, and had picked up a nub of chalk out of habit.

"Ray, are you sure you understand? This is vital. There's only one way we can know anything. Consciousness. Subjective awareness. If we take away all consciousness, if we take away all subjective awareness—"

"We have no way of knowing anything. I get it."

"Thus, the claim that a stand-alone objective world exists independent of our awareness—"

"Can never be verified," Ray had conceded.

"Skeptics who argue 'the subjective is unreliable' are delusional. It's the 'objective' that cannot be verified."

"So the universe is one big shared illusion?"

"Perhaps. In any event, we can dismiss skeptics who claim that subjective experiences play no valid role. They're simply wrong. All science rests on subjective observation. No scientist ever conducted an experiment without being involved subjectively."

Ray had been unable to rebut the argument. He had listened as his mentor continued.

"Skeptics make a dubious claim. They equate consensus with objective truth. That is an error, my friend."

"Yes. And last night—"

"In the matter discussed last night, the near-death experience, skeptics argue solely on the basis of consensus. They claim that their consensus—which argues that near death experiences are artifacts of brain activity—stands as objective truth."

"But that is merely subjective," Ray added.

"Exactly. We can say the same thing. We've accumulated consistent near-death reports. We have a consensus as well." He had tapped his pipe on the wastebasket for emphasis before opening a new pouch of tobacco and refilling his pipe with the fresh blend. Ray recalled the questions he had asked the professor: "What about people who experience near death but don't see anything? Or those who see only black? Or those who don't know what they see?"

"Evidence shows the experience has a strong ideational component. Most accounts describe a world of thought forms. Thoughts become visible."

"And those who only see black?" Ray had pressed.

"A black cloud or veil is a common thought form. Black energy blocks out unwanted thoughts, perceptions, or memories. When a person doesn't wish to see a thought or a memory they slap a black cloud over it."

"Hysterical blindness?"

"That's a good analogy."

A student had tiptoed into the office to deliver faculty mail. He had dumped letters into the mail slot, and then had beat a hasty retreat as Sherpa had bounded after him, snapping at his cuffs. The professor had found the drama amusing.

That morning Ray had not wanted to lose his train of thought, so he had pressed on. "Are you saying that people who experience near death see both the physical world *and* mental images?"

"It would appear they exist in two realms simultaneously. So-called experts are unable to explain these mental images."

Ray had felt a twinge of remorse. The prior evening's betrayal lurked off stage. That morning, though he had not been totally on the same page with his mentor, he felt they had reestablished rapport. Maybe he had not lost his thesis adviser. Ray had tested the waters. "About my dissertation—"

"Can't really help," Kidner had replied curtly. "I'm leaving the University."

Though Ray had been shocked by the abrupt announcement, he had known there was no point in arguing or pleading.

"I've gleaned all I can from Western philosophy. Perhaps I'll visit Asia before I'm too old to travel."

"Buddhists believe the physical world is an illusion, don't they?"

"The good-natured fellow who sat under the Bodhi tree came up with a number of intriguing ideas."

Were congratulations in order? Ray had wondered. Had his mentor spent his life pursuing philosophy—only to come up empty-handed? Had he planned to travel halfway around the globe for a fresh start? Ray had been too stunned to offer either congratulations or condolences.

The professor had sat silently, embracing Ray with a calm expression. The conversation had concluded; the relationship had ended. Though Ray had fumbled about in an attempt to express some sort of farewell, his efforts had been to no avail. With one last glance at Sherpa, he had shuffled out of the office.

Now, many years later, he wondered how much he had contributed to the professor's decision to retire and travel. Kidner had needed young colleagues with whom he could forge new ideas. Ray had been a promising student. But there was no doubt that Ray's inability to follow Kidner up the steep trail of epistemology had discouraged the old man. Ray felt a deep pang of regret that hollowed out his gut. Kidner had attempted to share something of great value and Ray had failed to grasp his kindness.

* * *

When Ray looked up, he found Alice awake, watching him.

"Perhaps you're no longer so certain I'm wrong?" she said.

"I'd forgotten a lesson a professor once taught. It was nothing."

Outside the cabin, a Jack Terrier barked. Ray hurried to the window and looked outside but the fog obscured his view. A shiver overtook him. Something terribly odd was in play, and something sinister was trying to make its presence known. He faced Alice, his only companion in this strange world.

"I'm sorry," he said. "It was rude of me to call you Alice."

"If I remind you of Alice, call me Alice."

"But who are you?"

She responded with a line from Carroll's book, "*I can't explain myself... because I'm not myself.*"

Was she mocking him?

"I don't mind that we quarrel," she said. "I quite like it, because it helps you. Did you know that helping others is the most important thing a person can do?"

"Are you mocking? Is this your way—"

"*You're so easily offended, you know!*" Another quote. "*Keep your temper,*" she said as she curtsied.

It occurred to Ray that she aimed to drive him mad.

"You ask me who I am?"

He nodded.

"Do you remember when Alice, the girl in the story, tried to fancy what the flame of a candle looked like after the candle is blown out?"

Ray was in no mood for riddles. And yet he was unable to dismiss the puzzle: what *did* the flame of a candle—after the candle is blown out—have to do with him?

"It's a clue," she said. "But it's getting late and it may be easier if I illustrate."

She slipped a protective cover off a screen that Ray had failed to notice. She began to sketch and animate with what Ray assumed was an electronic wand hidden in her palm. She illustrated a sphere that collapsed down to a point. Then the sphere ballooned to fill the screen, before collapsing and then expanding one more time.

"The sphere represents your conscious awareness. Some might call it your space."

She dug a green cat's-eye marble out of the box of toys and placed it on the stone hearth. Flames flickered and reflected off its glassy spherical surface.

"Narrow your focus, put your attention into the marble. Concentrate. Now place your attention on the trees outside. GO."

His awareness or "space" ballooned. He couldn't see the trees from his position—not with his eyes—but he found them with his attention, with his awareness. He knew where they were.

"You can make a conscious decision to expand or contract

your awareness. It responds to your will."

Turning back to the screen, she illustrated a crude, but proportionally accurate, human body. She illustrated a sphere of conscious awareness.

"The conscious spirit can locate itself—here, here, or here." The last "here" was in a position superimposed over the body. "This is the spirit or soul. Who you really are."

She moved the "sphere of consciousness" around the screen. "You can view from any position. The amount of space you view varies. You can be very tiny, inside a marble. You can be stuck in the middle of a head. Or you can be vast—and your body appears as a tiny sliver in the sphere of your awareness."

"I'm not able to do that," he countered.

"Because you identify with the body."

She illustrated a sphere of consciousness and "poured" the white sphere into the dark human form. The body turned light gray, newly radiant with the presence of consciousness.

"The conscious being or soul can pervade any form. It may consider it is that form. It identifies with the form. It plays the 'game' of *being a body*."

Ray was not buying it. "We see the body and know it is real. We can't see spirit or consciousness."

"You must learn the difference between that which is seen and that which sees. That which is observed is material. The observer is immaterial. Two different classes with different properties."

"A conscious observer is immaterial?"

Though she had covered this point previously she understood it was a very difficult concept to grasp. "This is where science goes amiss," she said. "Remember what your mentor taught? Scientists do not understand the observer and the observer's immaterial nature. This lack of understanding sabotages the entirety of science."

"Yes, a professor once said something like that." *How did she know about Kidner?* Alice and the professor, separately, had both assaulted his reality. Perhaps they were prompting him to discover an elusive truth. He was beginning to care less and less about science, less and less about debate and logic, and more and more about how it applied to his dire situation on this mountain. *What was she trying to teach him?*

"When we have a spirit composited with a body, the result is a human person," she said, pointing to the screen.

"Wait," Ray said. "Go back. You said that as a spirit I'm nothing?"

"Not exactly. It's not like you have no existence. Rather, think of yourself existing but as a No Thing. Not matter. Not energy."

Ray tried to imagine being a "No Thing." It wasn't easy. In fact, it was the most difficult concept he had ever encountered. The problem wasn't intellectual, but emotional. *How could his life, his feelings, ideas, loves, and memories be reduced to no thing?*

The mere thought prompted extreme vertigo and nausea. Terror skirted the edges of his awareness. It was the kind of terror that chased brave men from their dreams drenched in sweat, their hearts pounding. The light dimmed; the room grew dark. Clouds of black energy obscured Ray's vision. He was being drawn toward a dark abyss.

12

Randi, Hal, and Chase reached the lobby, one floor above the cafeteria. Randi apologized, "Hal, I'm sorry. I blew it. I had no idea Seidman was on the Board."

"I'm sure he understands. He would expect anyone to be a little stressed if…" Hal failed to find a tactful way to say *your son is dying.*

"Listen, you could probably use some sleep," he said.

Randi's defenses sprung up. Did Hal think she was senile? She studied his puppy-dog eyes and found nothing but kindness in his expression.

"I *am* starting to get a wee bit blurry around the edges," she admitted. "I'm about as much help as a lifeguard in the Sahara. I need to find a place—"

Chase pressed a hotel key card into her palm. "We reserved a room at the Marriott, under your name. Get some rest. We'll meet up later."

Hal hugged Randi—a comforting bear hug. As Chase escorted Randi to the exit, she feared the emotional damn she had engineered was about to break, allowing her *emotions to burst forth. How long could she keep her secret?*

"The driver will know the hotel," she said, guiding Randi into the backseat of a waiting taxi.

* * *

Five minutes later, the taxi slowed as traffic thickened. Randi stared out the window. They were passing through a gentrified section of town. The street was lined with two-story brick buildings adorned with decorative awnings. Charming architecture housed stylish enterprises: clothing boutiques, upscale shoe stores, florists, trendy restaurants, and corporate retail outposts.

She had never felt more disconnected from the flow of life, never so detached from the bustling crowd. On a typical day, the commotion of commerce would have raised her spirits, but today it felt sacrilegious. She studied the faces of passersby and wondered how many secretly grieved. How many passed through life with heavy hearts, present in the flesh but missing in the spirit.

Was she a chronic outsider? Or was she simply lonely, as a result of being trapped in her own mind? The shoppers on the street may have formed a temporary tribal brotherhood, but they, too, were innately separate, inhabiting personal island universes.

She wondered if she would feel differently if her ex-husband, Frank, shared her grief. Yes, she chuckled to herself, she would feel much worse. She hadn't seen him in ten years. Maybe it was best that way. After all, if Ray were to regain consciousness, most likely he would not want to see his father. Perhaps she only wanted Frank to share the terrible burden of terminating life support but most likely he would only make things worse.

For years, she had attributed his boorish behavior to the suffering that he must have experienced as a child in an abusive home. She imagined he had been too young and too little to defend himself against the tyranny. The blows he suffered must have twisted his character, she reasoned. During their marriage, she had tried to silence his angry inner voice but had failed. She was no match for the dark voices that haunted him.

Her failure had left her wondering if some people were inherently vicious, regardless of circumstances. Was there such a thing as inherent evil? She was disturbed by the thought that no matter what she did, Frank would have raised an angry fist against the world.

She tuned out the world passing by outside the cab and slipped into a reverie. She recalled a friend's poetic musings: *were we all magicians assigned to turn a portion of the world's lead into gold? Were we tasked with transmuting coarseness into beauty?*

She smiled ruefully at the thought her ex had been an evil magician spewing a toxic potion on others. The unpleasant thought motivated her to still her mind's noisy chatter. She closed her eyes and when she opened them again, the taxi pulled up in front of the hotel. A doorman with a pleasant smile and a slight limp carried her bag and escorted her to the registration desk.

Fifteen minutes later, alone in her room, she collapsed on the bed. Before sleep could grace her with peace, guilt paid an unscheduled visit. She realized that she had been feeling sorry for herself and she had wallowed in the pain of her loneliness, when, in truth, she was not alone. Father McCarty and Dr. Seidman had offered help. Chase and Hal had cared for her. She had failed to appreciate the kindness shown to her, she had been ungrateful and was now ashamed. As she drifted into sleep, she vowed to remedy her oversight.

13

Ray found himself sinking into the quicksand of unconsciousness. But then, abruptly, something halted his descent. It was Alice: she had wrapped him in a compassionate hug. As swirling clouds of black energy dissipated and the cabin sanctuary rematerialized, she released him.

Embarrassed, Ray reassured Alice his tumble into darkness was not her fault. She had not failed him as a teacher. "I should have done more to control my fear," he admitted.

As he surveyed his surroundings, he found himself suspended in a globe of otherworldly light emanating from Alice.

"I almost lost you," she confided. "The candle almost went out."

Still rattled, Ray glanced around. In spite of the Alice's glow, the room had not changed. It was as it had been before he plummeted into the abyss. Outside, the storm continued to darken the sky, though the faintest tinge of morning light broke through the trees.

During his tumble into darkness, a mind-blotting terror had created a psychic trauma from which he doubted he could recover. Though there were no external signs, he felt as if he had been gravely wounded.

Alice smiled with gentle sympathy. "*Mad, isn't it?*"

"*Puzzling, and a bit curious,*" he replied.

Though he tried to steady his heartbeat with deep controlled breathing, the panic persisted. He wanted to run but his urge to flee was tempered by the lingering dark that obscured his escape route.

"Doubt. It's a curse, is it not? Was there something you didn't understand?"

Of course there was, he admitted silently. There was little he did understand. Nothing was what it appeared to be. He yearned to rip off the veil of confusion clouding his vision to reveal the secrets that were just out of reach. Maybe the key was getting to know Alice, getting to know her motivation.

"Do you hike often in these woods?" he asked, as though wanting to engage in chitchat.

Alice titled her head with mock surprise. "You went and changed the subject. Are you frightened of what you might learn if we push ahead?"

He felt he had no option but to follow her chosen topic. "Okay, if the spirit is not the body, what happens when the body dies?"

"The spirit or soul separates."

"What happens to the soul without a body? Does it lose its ability to perceive? Does its awareness fade away?"

"Why would it?" Alice crossed to the screen and began to sketch. "Imagine a car. No, something more substantial: an armored tank. Imagine that inside the tank there are display screens, and those screens receive signals from video cameras mounted outside."

She sketched interior and exterior views of the tank.

"Now imagine dozens of sensors: temperature gauges; altitude gauges; gauges that measure water pressure, engine heat, speed, compass direction. They transmit data to a central processor where it can be accessed by the driver."

He wasn't sure where her illustration was taking them, but he nodded for her to continue.

"I'll make the analogy a little more clear. I'll place a body side-by-side with the tank. In the tank, the central processor is a computer. In the body, the central processor is the brain. Both central processors receive information from sensors."

Ray nodded.

"Let's continue the analogy." She animated a driver climbing into the tank. Then she sketched a "sphere of awareness" pouring into the body. "Just as the driver climbs inside the vehicle, so a soul enters the flesh body. The driver operates the tank, the soul operates the body."

It was a simple analogy: in both cases, a driver, who was not intrinsically part of the mechanical vehicle, entered and took over the controls. As she continued sketching, she explained her model.

"The driver can activate the tank's automatic pilot, if he wishes. He can climb up through the hatch and scan the countryside as the tank rolls along. Or he can run alongside the tank and operate it with a remote control device."

"Okay," Ray said, without fully understanding.

"Here's the point. We have a mechanical vehicle. And it

possesses complex sensing, processing, and operational capabilities. But those functions are separate from the driver's abilities. We have a dual system. The tank and the driver are not identical, right?"

"Yes, of course," Ray replied. "The driver makes decisions and operates the vehicle, like when we drive a car. We do not think we are the car."

"I'll admit it's a crude analogy when we apply it to body and soul. Yet it illustrates the idea that we have a body, which possesses certain properties. And they are physical properties, which differ from the driver, which is the soul that exists separate from the body. The soul, as a driver, makes decisions. It exercises free will."

Ray was mesmerized by her tutelage. He followed her down an unknown path doing his best to engage his critical faculties.

"Are you paying attention?" Alice prodded. "If we're going to make progress—"

"I'm good. Go on."

"Okay. This is important. You can study the body and the brain, its central processor, and discover its mechanics and its various functions. But, no matter how deep you dig you'll not discover free will. You don't discover a conscious agent exercising deliberate intention. Those qualities reside with the spirit."

"Spirit controls flesh—"

"Right. A soul can operate the body—but can only make it perform tasks that are mechanically possible. It can't make the body fly, at least not with very good results."

"The ability to fly is what I need right now," Ray commented.

Alice studied him for a beat. Would he continue explaining…?

"Just kidding. Go on," he said.

"The body lacks free will. It lacks the ability to reason. You will not find those qualities in a body. A body without a soul is a mechanical, stimulus-response machine."

Alice's analogy made perfect sense, but Ray's mind had turned dull and sluggish. *Was he losing control?* His thoughts strayed back to the dark terror that had overwhelmed him. That was not her fault, he reasoned. Rather, that fear most likely must had been his hidden traveling companion for a very long time. Ray forced his attention back to Alice, trying to keep crazy thoughts at bay.

Alice, seemingly oblivious to Ray's interior struggle, was playfully piloting the illustrated tank and the illustrated body.

"What about memory?" Ray interjected.

"The vehicle has a mechanical memory, a central computer which stores input from the senses. Mechanical memory is stored data that can be accessed and processed."

Ray considered the idea.

"We can use mechanical memory to create stimulus-response routines. For example, learning to ride a bicycle or hit a baseball or ice skate. After we learn through practice and repetition, we no longer think about our actions. We have created a stimulus-response pattern, so the mechanics become automatic. This is true of many physical tasks."

"Of course the body is pre-programmed with a genetic

code built up over eons," he added. "It arrives with pre-installed software, with programs that direct the construction of proteins and cells. These genetic programs construct and operate basic biological systems."

"True. That's mechanics. But the memory of the driver differs. Recall the analogy and how the driver's memory is not identical to the vehicle's memory. The vehicle computer records and stores physical data derived from sensors. The driver, on the other hand, exercises free will and tracks a moment to moment stream of consciousness."

She piloted a matchbox car in a circle on the table, demonstrating as she continued to lecture.

"Think about driving a car. You make decisions: where to go and how to get there. You remember your drive. Your memory includes how you operated the car—how you turned the wheel, pressed the brake, accelerated and so forth. You recall sights you observed going past outside the car. You have a stream of consciousness recall that differs from the car's mechanical memory."

"In that example, a dual system makes sense," he said.

She crossed to the screen. "The soul's memory is captured in mental energy. The soul creates and collects mental images of all its experiences."

"But scientists only consider the body's computer, the brain and the nervous system."

"That's where they go wrong. They refuse to recognize that we have two separate-but-linked systems working in tandem."

Ray repeated the idea to make sure he grasped it. "The

brain functions as a mechanical computer and lacks free will or intention. The spirit or soul exercises free will and possesses a memory separate from the brain's memory. Do I have that right?" Ray asked.

"Correct. Spirit creates energy pictures, copies of the physical world. The mind is made up of these images. When you daydream, for example, you view your mental pictures. When a soul departs the body, the mind goes with it. The soul's memory remains with the soul."

"I'm beginning to understand. But this isn't science—"

"Scientists are like a primitive tribe. They attribute magical powers to the brain, as if it is a black box out of which consciousness magically appears. They cannot explain how neurons and synapses create consciousness. They've never come close to an explanation, they simply claim miracles flow out of the black box."

Ray recalled the standard sound bite: "We don't know what happens or how it happens *but we assume…*"

"If not for the prejudices of materialism, dualism would be the dominant model. Science has been hijacked and dragged into the swamp. Scientists have gone quite mad."

Ray posed a question he could not dismiss from his mind, "If a soul leaves the body, as you describe, does it get another body? You know, reincarnation."

"If your overcoat wears out, do you purchase a new one? If your car rusts or the engine fails, do you buy another?"

"A body is different. It *is* a person."

"You make the mistake of thinking *I am the body*."

She grabbed a toy replica of a Volkswagen Beetle. "The

driver may become emotionally attached to his car. His sense of self-worth and identity may become tied to that object. But no matter how much the driver loves his car, we do not consider him to be the car."

"But no one has witnessed a soul get out of a body."

Alice tilted her head and eyed Ray critically. Her look penetrated and frightened him.

"What's wrong?" he replied. "Okay, some people claim they've had the experience—"

"There's a difference between material and immaterial realms. Spirit is immaterial. One does not see a soul in the same way one sees a body. But one can see the energy thought forms that a spirit or soul projects. Mental images. Remember?"

"*That's what a psychic medium sees?* Mental energy pictures of thoughts?"

"The spirit surrounds itself with energy images. Not a good idea, but it does. A soul accumulates energy images like adding shirts, sweaters, and overcoats, layer after layer. It becomes shrouded in layers of subtle energy. Remember the spirit is a No Thing—"

Ray felt a tinge of panic as he recalled the last time they discussed his being a No Thing. He didn't want a second run at it.

Alice reached into the cardboard box and selected three Matchbox cars: a VW, a '57 Chevy, and a Mercedes 450sl. "The cars are like the body—"

"And the soul changes bodies," he added.

"That idea could be very important. You might disentangle from burdens you carry."

"How's that?"

"Souls are burdened. They carry the cumulative record of their entanglement with the physical universe. With all this baggage, souls cannot see clearly. First, they must realize they're a soul. What point would there be in trying to free a soul from entanglement—if the soul doesn't even know that it exists?"

"But—"

"If you don't know you're trapped, what could possibly motivate you to free yourself?"

"This has been one mad tea party, hasn't it?" he joked. A line from *Adventures in Wonderland* came to him: "*I don't want to go among mad people.*"

"Oh, you can't help it. *We're all mad,*" Alice fired back with a wink.

14

Hal and Chase rode the elevator in silence. The time for small talk had passed. Hal's frustration overflowed, "Not sure I can continue in limbo. Seems the doctors are just waiting for something to happen. Wish they would do something."

"Uh oh, what are you up to?" She knew that Hal craved action. It was not in his nature to simply wait.

"Ray and I met this odd fellow who lives in a cabin on the other side of Gold Hill. We hiked up that way on occasion. Sometimes we stopped and visited. Nice enough guy, though into a whole lot of superstition. Maybe that's what we need now—crazy wisdom. We need a witch doctor or a shaman. Want to come with me?"

"One of us should stay."

"Makes sense. I'll be back."

* * *

Chase dialed her boss. When he came on the line, she asked for time off. She would not be in tomorrow, or the following day. She would be missed. Ray used to joke that she made the world a cleaner place—she sold industrial water treatment and waste removal systems. So for a few days, the world would be a little a less tidy.

Ray had also joked that cleanliness was next to godliness. At this moment, she would have traded some cleanliness for a little godliness, if it meant she could help Ray. For the first time since Ray had been admitted to ICU, she was alone with him. Yet she found the hospital annoying. If you needed some quiet to work on a problem, it was the worst possible venue. And she was working on a major problem: *Ray was dying.*

She closed her eyes and tried to subdue the mental clatter. She recalled their nightly ritual—every evening she and Ray "cleaned house," sweeping away mental baggage that had accumulated during the day. They had come to realize that the people they encountered during the day were eager to off-load: they needed to dump their problems, desires, opinions, emotions, suffering, and complaints. By the time Chase and Ray arrived home, they carried this human burden, whether consciously or unconsciously. While an outsider might view their ritual as nothing more than a lively chat, the couple realized they were exorcizing psychic debris.

Now that she was finally alone with Ray, she wondered if she could slip into his stream of consciousness and recreate that ritual. Would she be able to help him unburden and find his way home? Though she quickly dismissed that fantasy, she knew that hope, no matter how farfetched, was far better than accepting defeat. She also knew that some accidents were not really accidents. Many "victims" were predisposed to mishaps: they were heading for a crack-up long before disaster struck. But that was not the case with Ray. He wasn't that kind; he was a long-term player. He had even delayed setting their wedding date because he wanted to "get his ducks in a row." He wanted to peer down the tunnel of time and know with certainty that success was ensured. He would not, consciously or subconsciously, plant the seeds of his own demise or booby-trap his own future.

So what had happened? What did she know? He had been driving over a mountain pass in a light snow flurry, something he had done hundreds of times previously. This time he was bringing her the good news that the contract was signed, the funds approved. At long last, his "ducks were in a row." Was God so malevolent, such a bullying tease, that he would entice a man to reach for success and then, when it was within reach, chop off his outstretched hand? Chase could not imagine a universe rigged in such a malevolent way.

Besides, she knew Ray believed in a rational universe, a universe that had evolved out of chaos into the complex wonder we observed through telescopes and microscopes. He believed every question had an answer; one just had to ask. And ask he did. He asked so many questions he drove her batty. He was like a precocious kid who discovers the infinite regress of *Why? Why? Why?* It was no longer necessary for him to voice the *Why?* It was a given, a question ingrained in his personality.

Now, Chase realized, Ray had stumbled upon a *Why?* to which there was no good answer. He was cocooned in the numbing silence of a coma, on the doorstep of the eternal silence of death. He was in a place beyond questions and answers, where the only things that mattered were *decisions*—such as the decision to be or not to be. As much as she knew that she couldn't make the decision for Ray, she tried.

* * *

At the hotel, Randi, refreshed after a two-hour nap, phoned Father McCarty to ask for directions to his parish. She had not embraced his theology, and for that she felt no regret, but she did regret not having been more open to his pastoral outreach. She felt the same regrets when it came to Seidman: she had been rude and wanted to make amends.

Her new outlook had gelled during her nap. In the state between dreaming and waking, she had revisited her messy divorce and recalled the time when Ray, buffeted by his parents' stormy emotions, had offered heartfelt advice. She had snapped back with a curt response: he was too young to know anything about divorce. Ray, only eleven and on edge emotionally, had delivered an impassioned lecture: she should listen when someone offered help, because help might come from unexpected places, even from those who knew nothing about divorce. Even from kids.

In the years since, her son's impassioned words resurfaced in her memory from time to time. *She should listen when help was offered.* Though Father McCarty did not know her heart when it came to religion and though Seidman offered theories she found repugnant, both had offered help that she had failed to acknowledge. After stripping away theory and theology, one brute fact remained—helping hands had been extended. Ray had taught her to grasp those outstretched hands.

Father McCarty came on the line. "I'm glad you called. I wasn't sure we would speak again. I was afraid I hadn't provided much comfort."

She had made the correct decision. Father McCarty was a caring man. His offer of help was genuine.

"Then I got to thinking," he continued, "there's someone you should meet, an old friend of mine. Where are you?"

"Downtown Marriott."

"Do you mind if I send him over to see you?"

"I suppose I don't mind. But who—"

"This is a bit irregular. He researches the paranormal. The Church is not officially into—"

"The work of the Devil?" she said, poking fun.

"That captures the situation quite well." The twinkle in his eye came through his voice. "In my line of work, even though we have a rich tradition of mystical insights, cavorting with such folks can be bad for job security."

"Father."

"Yes?"

"I want to tell you I appreciate how much you care. You know, for one person to help another…"

"Yes…"

"It's special. My son Ray taught me that."

"Your son is very wise. He has a lovely mother, with a heavenly sense of humor."

***

Twenty minutes later, Les Carson phoned from the lobby. Randi met him in the coffee shop. He ordered a Coke. She ordered apple pie a la mode and coffee, decaf.

The first thing she noticed about Les was the lapel pin on his dark blue suit—*a pink unicorn*. Her gaze lingered on the mythical figure with a horn protruding from its equine forehead.

"Pink unicorns don't exist, except in literature and imagination," he informed her. "Thus, skeptics take pleasure in ridiculing paranormal research as the equivalent of pink unicorns—non-existent. The pin is a mocking salute to their cynicism."

Randi appreciated his self-deprecating humor.

"I'm starting the *Pink Unicorns Club*," he said. "Would you like to join? You would be the first charter member." His smile bubbled up from the depths of a reservoir of good nature. He was a man on good terms with humor. But, at times, he was known to adopt a standoffish posture for professional reasons. He explained how skeptics approached him with an open hand and easy smile before launching humorless and scathing attacks.

Skeptics, he noted, banded together in clubs, not to study the paranormal, as they claimed, but rather to form mini-mobs that would belittle anyone trying to understand the paranormal. They used the media to attack the research. Their attacks should be designated as hate speech, but they justified their vitriol as science and thus escaped censure.

However, if one checked closely, Les explained, little or no science took place within these groups, only expressions of prejudice.

Les, recognizing that Randi was neither a radical skeptic nor a naïve believer, loosened his tie and relaxed. He found pleasure in discussing his work with those who were unbiased. "Father McCarty explained your situation. He felt I might offer reassurance."

"He's a kind man. Have you known him long?" she asked.

"We were roommates in the seminary. Then we turned in different directions."

"What happened?"

"Our final year in the seminary we both landed jobs at a hospital in Chicago. Mercy Hospital on the South Side, close to the lake. They called us orderlies though we were little more than glorified gofers. We transported patients, equipment, and supplies. And we transported the recently deceased to the morgue."

He paused, afraid the word "deceased" might upset or offend Randi. There was no change in her expression, so he continued. "At night, in the hospital, we confronted death, we went face to face with the Reaper. The call would usually come over the intercom. We would wheel a gurney to the room of the patient who had passed. Nurses would leave a large black plastic bag for the body and a tag we were to affix to the toe of the corpse. That was our job—tag 'em and bag 'em."

Les was deeply affected by one memory in particular: "One night, our errands started in the usual manner. Then something quite out of the ordinary happened. McCarty and I entered a room… we were supposed to remove the body of a deceased woman."

"That must have been uncomfortable," Randi noted.

"All at once, we both felt a strong presence. We didn't see a ghost or anything like that, but the presence was… unmistakable. The woman who had passed seemed to be trying to get our attention. Like a ghost but not one you could see."

"A little scary."

"No. Not really. Just… odd. It seemed like she wanted to know what we were doing. She was looking over our shoulders, all fussy and bossy. If this happened to just one of us, we would have brushed it off as imagination. But we both felt exactly the same thing. As you can imagine, it made quite an impression on both McCarty and me."

He sipped his Coke and then continued, "The next day, we met in the chapel to sort out what it all meant. You know, divinity students as philosopher kings. Sitting in the chapel, looking at the image of Christ on the cross, it was clear to me that the crucifixion and resurrection assured us that we survive death. We're immortal souls."

"Yes. So did anything else happen?" she asked.

"A couple weeks later, we're in the chapel discussing the Resurrection, sorting out the misconceptions. You know, corpses rising out of graves like zombies. We got to laughing over that film—"

"Night of the Living Dead," Randi interjected.

"Yes. McCarty slipped away. I hadn't noticed. He flopped down in a pew, out of sight. When I looked back, he rose up stiff as a corpse, imitating a zombie. It was absurd and terribly inappropriate. But you know how you laugh when something isn't really funny, because it triggers something? Pretty soon we're both popping up out of the pews pretending to be zombies rising out of the grave. We're cracking up, because we needed a release from the tension of that experience with the deceased lady's ghost."

He paused, sipped his coke. "We were laughing so hysterically we failed to notice a priest who walked past. But he noticed us. We got ourselves banned from the chapel for the entire semester."

Randi smiled at the idea of a young Father McCarty banned from the chapel.

"That day… it was clear to me that the most important questions concerned life beyond death. I wasn't certain the Church would give me the answers, but McCarty saw it differently. He was right, but, back then, I didn't know how to look. He remained a dear friend. We get together a few times a year."

"So, tell me, what have you found?"

"Our research focuses on continuity of consciousness."

"What's that?"

"Another way of saying life after death. We avoid the words spirit and soul, as they have accumulated negative connotations. Though what we traditionally call a soul is a consciousness that survives body death."

"So you study spiritual things, but don't advertise it?"

"We're trying to garner acceptance in the scientific community. It's perhaps a foolish goal. Maybe science and religion should be kept separate, but ultimately they study the same thing. The pretense that they are separate domains must eventually be dismissed. One day spiritual beliefs will be confirmed empirically."

"Science and religion will overlap?"

"There's no conflict between belief in spirit and science."

"What did Father McCarty think you would say to me that would provide comfort?"

"I believe he hoped I would convince you that continuity of consciousness is real. We have found proof in the near death experience."

Randi was suddenly distracted. Dr. Seidman arrived, unexpected. "I'm sorry if I'm interrupting," he said. "Chase thought I might find you here. I wanted to apologize."

"No, *I* want to apologize," Randi said, leaping to her feet. "In fact, you were on my list of official apologies. Please, be seated. This is Les Carson."

A forced politeness tempered their greeting.

"You know each other?" Randi asked.

"We haven't met, but I'm familiar with his work."

"Come, sit down. How can we apologize standing up? Would you like a cup of coffee?"

"With cream, please." He slid into the booth as Randi summoned the waitress.

"Les and I were talking about the near death experience," Randi said.

"Oxygen deprivation," Seidman interjected.

"That explanation doesn't add up," Les said. "We have cases that don't include oxygen deprivation. It must be set aside as *the* cause."

Dr. Seidman nodded almost imperceptibly.

"We find different kinds of trauma precipitate the NDE event. We must ask what they all have in common. One must account for *all* the data. One must find a common factor. And there is one common factor—serious threat to the survival of the body."

"So the bottom line…" Seidman prompted.

"If we have both soul *and* body, we would expect to find instances when a soul separates from the body. And that's *exactly* what we find. No matter what kind of trauma precipitates the NDE, the person experiences a separation, an out-of-body experience. When the survival of the body is threatened, the soul departs."

Seidman nodded. Randi wondered if he was agreeing or silently protesting.

"Any type of trauma producing imminent death can cause the NDE. Oxygen deprivation is just one type. And, in some instances, the out-of-body experience takes place without actual physical trauma—exactly what one would expect if spirit and body are truly separate."

"All explained by altered brain chemistry."

"Another argument that fails," Les countered. "Brain chemistry does not explain viewing physical events from positions outside the body."

"What do you mean?" Randi asked.

"For example, subjects report looking down on the doctors operating on their body. Or they describe their family in the waiting room. Or they describe people and events at distant locations. Neither the brain nor any of its sense organs are in a position to view from those vantage points."

"Imagination cobbles together old memories to make new stories," Seidman added tersely.

"Doesn't fit the evidence. Subjects describe events they've never seen previously. Often details match unique events that took place on only one occasion."

"Extraordinary claims require extraordinary evidence," Dr. Seidman stated, as though the axiom trumped all discussion.

The phrase had been tossed in Les' face too many times before for it to unsettle him. "That's just it," he said. "The claims aren't extraordinary. Similar claims appear throughout recorded history. It's all very ordinary. Only in the narrow paradigm of materialism do such claims appear extraordinary." He barely suppressed a smirk.

"Was something funny?" Randi asked.

"Skeptics make extraordinary claims when they try to dismiss the evidence. Some are humorous, and absurd."

The waitress, eavesdropping, refilled Les's Coke. He was just getting warmed up. "I'll give you an example of the poor science found in skeptics' circles."

"I don't defend those groups." Seidman objected.

"Don't take it personally. I'm merely presenting common misconceptions used to dismiss serious research. For example, the myth that free will is an illusion: the idea the brain makes decisions without our knowledge."

"That's no myth," Seidman objected. "Experiments demonstrate the brain executes decisions without our conscious knowledge. After a delay, those decisions become conscious. We fool ourselves into thinking we make conscious decisions. We fool ourselves into believing we possess free will."

"I know the work you reference. It was not valid. A couple psychologists tried to defend a weak theory with faulty conclusions and failed. Others repeated the claim without checking the research. A false claim became 'established' science. If they had checked the original work, they would have known experiments failed to show any such thing."

"If what you say is true, it's a black mark against science, but in the long run—"

"Long run? How long shall we allow prejudice to determine the path of science?"

Randi enjoyed the back-and-forth banter, as it took her mind off her troubles—but her thoughts soon drifted back to Ray.

"If you're right," Randi said, "My son, in a way we don't yet understand, remains conscious, though unable to communicate."

Seidman looked away with disgust. For him this was carnival talk.

"There's no reason to show disrespect," Randi said. "I made that mistake with you. My son taught me that if someone tries to help, even if they don't have all the answers, it pays to listen, because their desire to help is the most important thing. I don't know if Les has answers, but I'm not going to be rude."

"Pardon me, but I happen to know where he's going with

these ideas. The use of mediums is something I'll not con-done on my watch."

"I would never recommend a medium in situations like this," Les retorted.

"My friend, you're on a very slippery slope. Fortune-telling is not science."

"We don't engage in fortune-telling and you should not engage in sarcasm. Those who ridicule others simply show they're frightened."

"What frightens me is a psychic medium in my hospital."

"He said he has no plans to bring anyone to see Ray," Randi countered.

"Do you have any idea what a medium does?" Les asked Seidman.

"Commits fraud?"

"Mediums see the visual images you or I view when we remember something. It's a kind of memory. Close your eyes."

Randi closed her eyes. Seidman hesitated, but then acquiesced.

"See the image of a horse. See its color. Is it a thorough-bred? Or maybe a pony?"

Both Seidman and Randi nodded and opened their eyes.

"That's an image you can see," Les said. "Mediums see energy pictures like that. Those who experience near death report a rich world of thought forms and those images are not always their own. They seem to perceive the thoughts of others. Mediums are simply good at seeing mental energy."

"Can anyone do the same thing?" Randi asked.

"Good question. If souls project energy pictures to communicate, it would make sense that it's an ability we all possess. Perhaps a dormant ability."

The eavesdropping waitress raised her eyebrow: *you guys are out there*. When they looked up, she blushed and busied herself folding napkins.

"The problem we encounter," Les continued, "is the noise-to-noise signal ratio is very high."

"Noise-to-signal ratio?" Randi asked.

"Imagine watching six television shows at once. Then try to describe what you viewed."

Les had successfully conveyed his ideas to Randi but doubted he would ever say enough to convince the psychologist.

"Interesting theories," Seidman observed. "While many accept NDE reports as proof of an afterlife, the popularity of a belief does not attest to its accuracy."

"We're not talking belief, we're talking evidence," Les replied.

"Oh, it's one of the most ancient of all human beliefs," Seidman asserted.

Les swirled the ice in the bottom of his glass, conveying restraint. "Such beliefs are supported by experiences common for thousands of years."

"Pursue your line of inquiry. But understand—no mediums visit my hospital. Mrs. Carte, there would be no point in trying to discourage you from considering these ideas. But I hope you consider all options."

Randi could tell he was employing extraordinary effort to

pose as a reasoned person, while his objections were entirely visceral. She replied, "I don't have the luxury of tossing a single good idea. I want my son back. You two stay and sort out your differences."

As she stood, Les slipped her his business card emblazoned with a pink unicorn.

Seidman climbed out of the booth; he and Les were not about to convene a summit on the paranormal. Randi found the intense acrimony sad; but, she thought, that's human nature and scientists are human.

As she reached the door, the eavesdropping waitress shot her a supportive wink. Randi returned a smile as she stepped out onto the street. She decided to walk back to the hospital, after being locked in such close quarters. Maybe Les was on to something. Pink unicorns might not be real, but they were real in people's minds, and that was not something to be easily discarded.

15

"Reincarnation is a simple idea," Alice said, clearing the screen with her unseen wand. "It's only made to seem difficult by those—"

"Like me?" Ray interrupted.

"You are one of my more difficult students."

"So I'm officially your student?"

"I've not given up hope."

"I appreciate that."

"Either way, it doesn't matter. What you fail to learn from me, life will teach you—"

"I don't recall a prior life," he said. "Not a one."

"Lost memories will be recovered when you walk the path in earnest," she said. "That time has not yet come."

"So this is strictly remedial."

"An intervention. In the future, pay better attention and you'll not be so forgetful."

Ray chafed in response to her mock disdain for his ability.

"So I suppose you chair the wisdom department at a prestigious galactic university?" he quipped.

He regretted his attempted insult immediately. For all he knew, *he* was the arrogant one, suffering over-inflated pride. Perhaps his ego was the raw nerve she hammered. Maybe her purpose was not to taunt him. Instead, she might be drawing him out into the light so that he might discover lost wisdom. He sighed and signaled for her to continue.

"We start with duality," she went on, as if there had been no interruption. "If we start with a body and a soul, we find reincarnation is easy to understand." She sketched a body, and then added a glowing sphere that represented the spirit or soul.

"We've been here before. We're circling the same block," said Ray.

She said nothing.

"Sorry, go on."

"The soul inhabits the body and assumes the identity of that body."

The idea made sense, logically. But how was he supposed to wrap his mind around such a bizarre concept?

"At first a soul may simply float in the vicinity of the body." She illustrated, moving the sphere. "Initially, the spirit occupies more space than the body occupies. It is outside and inside at once. Eventually, however, spirit and body become entangled."

She illustrated the sphere blanketing the body and then dispersing like water into the contours of the body.

"Wait a minute," Ray said. "*How* are they connected?"

"The interface is the mind. Notice I didn't say the brain."

"So mind is the glue that binds spirit to the body?"

"Yes. Remember, the mind is comprised of mental energy forms created by the soul. A soul makes copies of everything it perceives, every second, in mental energy. This memory is not static like a photo but rather like a three-dimensional movie."

"Like a virtual reality movie or holographic movie."

"Yes. And the mental energy movie includes complex and multi-sense images of the body. The body is part of the energy movie. As you can imagine the film is very rich in information, beyond high definition."

With the wand, she shattered the sphere she had illustrated into a matrix, a network of lines conforming to the geometry of the body. The pattern reminded Ray of neural network illustrations or complex fractal patterns.

"The sphere of consciousness becomes a subtle mental body that docks with the coarser physical body. A subtle energy pattern forms the linkage."

"I follow. Mind conforms to the shape of the flesh body. Consciousness pervades the form. The subtle energy forms linkage so they operate as one. Like a hand in a sock puppet."

"Well, a better analogy," she said, "would be a pilot wave. Imagine a supertanker on the sea. And imagine an electromagnetic signal operating the controls from a distance. An invisible wave controls a huge massive object."

"But we were talking about reincarnation…" he said.

"Over a very long period of time, souls become entangled with one form after another, with one body after another. With each entanglement a soul creates an additional mental energy movie."

"It compulsively creates records of its entanglements."

"Exactly. Over time it accumulates a vast movie vault filled with mental energy records of many entanglements. These movies are comprised of very subtle energy. Buddhists called this the storehouse mind."

"And the movies just sit there?" he asked.

"When a soul hauling these old movies entangles with a new body, it superimposes some of the patterns over the new body. Some of the old pictures become entangled with the new body."

"Sounds like quite a mess."

"Yes, it truly is. Imagine the mental body—and its vast moving picture memory—docking with the new flesh body."

He tried his best to imagine the idea.

"This patterned mental energy body might even be thought of as a type of 'mental machinery' that works without our constant attention. Energy patterns, or old mental image movies, become part of the composite—spirit, mind, and body."

"Makes sense, conceptually," said Ray. "I'm familiar with autonomous systems forming composite, symbiotic systems. It happens frequently in biology."

"Then you now better understand Intelligent Design. Imagine a mental energy pattern impinging on the flesh body—that pattern becomes a 'designing' influence. Mental energy acts as a pattern or design."

"This is all very strange indeed," said Ray.

"The Watchmaker tinkering at his workbench is not an accurate metaphor. Instead, we might think of a Grand

Designer who creates sub designers, individual souls that entangle with material forms. Their minds entangle with substance and give it shape. Millions and millions of sub-designers mix subtle mental energy patterns with denser energy."

"This turns everything upside down," he said, feeling quite upside down himself. He was losing all sense of where he had been, where he was, and where he was headed. At this point, he relied on Alice for direction. By now, he knew she could care less about science. She was only interested in *his* progress. Just why this was so, he had no clue.

As he continued to reason through her lesson, he realized that cognitive scientists, neuroscientists, philosophers, and psychologists were of no help on his journey. They all shared a terrible error: they summarily dismissed dualism. Their texts shared a disclaimer: although brain-mind equivalence was *not* supported by empirical evidence, they would *assume* it was a fact. Their sleight-of-hand was self-imposed blind-ness. He needed sight, not blindness.

He queried Alice. "You said emotion played a role in our blindness."

"Emotion dictates 'don't look here' and causes us to avert our gaze. We have collected images of pain, loss, and trauma deep in our minds. We hide these images from view because they're scary. We protect ourselves by blacking out painful content."

Her words explained the black cloud that had engulfed him and closed down his awareness. And he knew those words had something to do with his missing memory. He wondered *what don't I wish to see?*

"Your mind is a storehouse filled with mental images of bad or painful experiences. You don't want to experience them again. You don't even want to see them. You block them."

"This is why few people remember a past life?"

"Right."

"But didn't one researcher claim that he found children who had recalled a past life? He also claimed that some had birthmarks that marked the location of past life injuries."

As she responded, she illustrated her ideas. "The storage mind contains energy pictures of past injuries. The energy images of a previously injured body part may affect the new body. An illness is sometimes simply an echo out of the past."

"So the past seeps into the present through these energy forms or patterns?"

"Constantly. The cumulative record of our pasts, buried behind a screen of black energy, seeps into the present."

"And we do not know because we've become amnesiacs."

"We avoid looking under rocks where past pain may lurk," she said. "There is a reason why reincarnation is so quickly dismissed—people are emotionally unprepared to look under rocks."

He wondered if he, too, was afraid to look under rocks. The more he probed, the darker the room became. *He was fading, going out like a candle.*

"Don't go there. Not yet," Alice warned.

The room brightened.

"Your past can be uncovered later."

"What just happened?"

"When we place our attention on past trauma, we may slip into unconsciousness," she explained. "The black cloud lulls us into sleep, like a narcotic."

Ray did not push for further explanation. He was not dying to unearth troubled memories. Yet, he could not let go entirely. "This hidden storehouse stuff… that's the subconscious?"

"Think of it as memories you would rather not recall."

"But scientists aren't the only ones that dismiss reincarnation. Christians don't accept the idea. They're very adamant that you live one and only one life."

"Christians believe in the existence of an immortal soul. Right?"

"Yes, go on."

"They speak of living only one life. But that does mean one flesh body."

"Wait. What do you mean?"

"The word for 'body' used in scripture was mistranslated from the Greek. The word did not mean flesh body. Rather it meant 'person.' And the actual person is the soul. And it is the soul that lives on with one life, with one eternal life. The soul enjoys a continuity of spiritual consciousness, quite beyond the life of one flesh body. After all, Christians believe in an afterlife."

"Okay. So we have only one life. But that one life is the life of the soul? That is not the same as one life as a flesh body."

"Correct. A soul exists throughout all time. One eternal life."

"Not one life as a flesh body."

A fleeting memory interrupted Ray's train of thought. He and Hal had visited an eccentric hermit living in a mountain cabin; over freshly brewed tea, they had discussed reincarnation. The hermit had opined, "*We're trapped on the wheel of birth and death, reincarnating again and again.*"

The memory prompted his question. "So when I die—"

"You will always be you," Alice interjected. "You may assume different bodies, just like an actor assumes roles. But, always, at all times, *you are you.* Unchanging soul. Whereas the identities of bodies are like a flowing river, always changing."

Ray was overcome with the same embarrassment he had experienced in the hermit's cabin. Reincarnation was a topic for fools. It was like talking about ghosts around the campfire. Alice anticipated his doubts…

"When we see ghosts, we are just seeing a projected mental image. That's all."

"I suppose there might be explanations…"

"There's one important truth. You are you, no matter what body you inhabit. When it is time, you move on. And you are still you. Maybe you enter a new vehicle. Changes of identity do not negate who you really are."

"Our past identities are not important?"

"Less important than realizing you're an immortal soul. The body may change, but you are always you."

"But our past must shape—"

"The past shapes the mind, the collection of mental energy forms. If not recognized and discarded, that mental energy debris can shape our present, for good or bad. But we're not the roles we play."

"I like who I am: Ray Carte. So, if you don't mind, I don't even want to talk anymore about reincarnation."

Alice smiled with a hint of irony. "Maybe we should wait before we order the cap and gown."

After a short beat, she asked, "Did the sage who lived in the mountain cabin speak about attachment?"

"If so, it meant little to me at the time," he replied.

"Attachment is the source of all suffering."

16

James Perspy, the mountain hermit that Ray and Hal had befriended, stroked his beard. "So, if Ray passes… are you going to be okay with that?"

The question caught Hal off guard. "No," he responded. "Not at all."

"That's unfortunate."

Hal slid out of his Jeep and quick-stepped after James, following him to a modest cabin nestled in a meadow a few miles west of Gold Hill. It was five hundred yards from a stream that flowed with snow melt from peaks straddling the Continental Divide. The structure had survived fifty winters of crushing snowdrifts; numerous times, the Chinook winds had battered and nearly leveled the home. At one time, it had seemed unlikely to survive another season, but then James had come along and rescued the outpost. Renovation had taken five months, the window of opportunity presented by the interlude between winters.

Hal did not know if James had gone to the trouble of securing legal claim to the property; most likely he was a squatter. Hal had never asked: *if James wasn't harming anyone, it wasn't any of his business.* That was the way mountain folk reasoned.

Though a recluse, James was not inhospitable. Ray and Hal had visited numerous times, shared pleasantries, and then hiked on. During one visit, Hal had been suffering from a nagging bruise that was the result of a climbing mishap. James had turned out to be quite an adept healer. The medicinal poultice he concocted proved miraculous: within twenty-four hours, the ache and debilitating stiffness had vanished. Hal and Ray had declared James their personal medicine man. Now Ray, in his present crisis, was in need of such a medicine man with truly unusual powers.

James led Hal inside his dwelling. Bookshelves lined the walls. They were filled with volumes on metaphysics, Buddhism, quantum physics, and holistic medicine. Hal, intimidated by the massive number of volumes and their arcane titles, was slow to reveal the reason for his visit. His simple, cautious nature was also a product of his upbringing.

Hal had been raised in Montana, the grandson of one of the last true horse doctors, a veterinarian who still made house calls, motoring out to ranches scattered throughout the county. As a boy, Hal had accompanied his grandfather on calls. Most days he would take the wheel of a classic 1950 Dodge, a beat-up old workhorse whose odometer had clocked well over two hundred thousand miles. Though, at that age, he could barely see over the dashboard, he had chauffeured the aging vet to appointments with sick, injured, or dying animals. Over the years, he had helped his grandfather treat hideously bloated steers, deliver foals, stitch lacerated horses, castrate bull calves, and vaccinate squealing pigs.

Hal's hands-on experience with sick creatures had given him a keen sense of the flow of life and death. He could handle suffering, blood, and death. Esoteric writings, on the other hand, belonged to a different world. He found pages of abstract pondering on life and death intolerable. He considered Big Ideas found in books had been squeezed crammed into too little space. In his eyes, such reductionism was unnatural.

Hal's attention came to rest on the bottom shelf of one bookcase. There he found a platoon of medical books standing at sloppy attention, their spines bent and their leather covers aged and cracked. Many times, Hal and Ray had speculated that James had once been a doctor; he had either quit or had been run out of the profession. They had never summoned the nerve to ask about his past.

A short time later they had taken up a guessing game: they speculated on what had happened to make James want to live alone in an isolated mountain cabin. He was no disturbed crackpot; he was a caring and gracious host who enjoyed his fellow man. His pointy beard, shoulder-length hair, and old-fashioned granny spectacles, along with his collection of esoteric texts, led Hal to joke that James was a reincarnated alchemist who had spent the fifteenth century in Prague turning lead into gold.

"Have you read *The Tibetan Book of the Dead?*" James asked, drawing Hal out of his reverie.

"Nope. Raised a Christian."

"You can still read, I hope. *The Book of the Dead* is a study in how to assist the recently departed move through the transition we call death."

"Ray isn't dead."

"Yet he is in a transition state. Listen up. In the post-mortem state the deceased remains aware of the emotions of the living. The manuscript warns that we should not allow clinging emotions to encumber the spirit as it makes its way to a new state."

"What does this have to do with Ray?"

"He's in a coma?"

"Right."

James stroked his beard thoughtfully. "In the comatose state one experiences much confusion. Some struggle with the decision to return."

"Wait. Back up. How does this work?"

"Tibetans believe that a person's thoughts at the moment of their death affect their transition. The journey might lead to enlightenment, it might lead to rebirth, or it might launch a journey into a hell region. The transition might be a kind of purgatory—they might have to purge burdens that hold them back, spiritually. After a person passes, a monk assists them by reading passages every day for forty-nine days."

"They communicate with the dead? How's *that*?"

"It's a form of prayer or meditation."

"That's one big-ass leap beyond…" Hal remarked, stepping back from the emotional edge on which he teetered. "We're getting a bit out there, James. Maybe we should put the old feet back on the ground."

James removed a teapot from his cast iron stove and poured hot water into cups filled with hand-tied bags of green tea. Hal was familiar with the ritual. Previously, they had engaged in the routine when he and Ray had visited. Today, after the tea service was meticulously laid out on the sawed-off mahogany table, they sat cross-legged in silence. Hal knew that if he hoped to solicit James' help he must abide the ritual, but the silence wore on like a brutal winter storm that refused to lift.

Finally, James asked, "What do the doctors say?"

"He took a blow to the head and remains unconscious. There was internal bleeding. They're worried about brain swelling. They don't feel the damage is permanent, but they said sometimes the system never comes back online."

"If it's best for Ray, can you let him go?"

"I can't imagine a way in which it would be best for him." He reflected. "And this isn't easy for his girlfriend and his mother."

James closed his eyes and appeared to meditate.

Hal wanted to leave. He realized that coming to see James was a mistake, an act of desperation. He had been pushed by the urge to *do something*—standing around the hospital was driving him crazy. But now he worried he had been hasty. Perhaps there was a good reason the doctors moved so agonizingly slow. Maybe doing nothing was better than doing something wrong.

"Drive me to the scene of the accident," James said.

"Oh, geez, James, that's okay," Hal replied. "Seems like I'd better get on back to town."

James locked a probing stare on Hal. "What did you say?"

Hal hated silent confrontations, and he knew he was up against a master. He caved, "We can take my Jeep."

$* * *$

The broken and battered sacrificial tree bled sap, which hardened in the sub-freezing cold. Snowflakes swirled, whitening the gash the runaway SUV had carved in the frozen soil.

James closed his eyes and ran a probing finger over the tree's wound.

Hal puffed nervous breaths, exhaling vapor trails. The crash site spooked him. James' weird behavior didn't help.

The hermit lowered into a squat at the base of the tree. With his eyes closed, he became oblivious to Hal's jittery presence. As if reading spiritual braille, he studied a world invisible to the human eye.

Hal kicked at a snowdrift and studied distant peaks where plumes of dry snow swirled against the blue sky. He wondered, cynically, if he had stepped into the Twilight Zone. He half-expected James to levitate. His decision to pay James a visit, he figured, must have been a side effect of sleep deprivation, as he was usually down-to-earth, a guy who knew how to take care of business. He vowed to indulge in a much-needed nap after he chauffeured James home.

Five minutes later—though it seemed an hour—James uncoiled his legs and rose. "Let's pay a visit to the hospital. I need to meet his mother and girlfriend. Maybe we can do something after all." As he turned to go, his boot struck a stray piece of debris buried in the snow.

"Leave it. It's junk, a piece of the truck or something," Hal called out.

Instead, James tracked the skid marks etched in the powdery snow. He blew away a dusting of icy crystals and uncovered the toy monk that had once dangled from Ray's rearview mirror. He fingered the icon and held it up for Hal to see.

Hal recognized it. "You gave that to him, didn't you?"

"I thought he tossed it. He didn't seem interested. How curious."

On the ride down the hill, Hal tried to entice James into revealing the visions he had just witnessed with his "inner eye."

James, skittish in the face of Hal's latent doubt, was not forthcoming. "Nothing much, Hal. I'm just entertaining a hunch. Call it intuition. I'm not sure Ray was ready to make a rapid departure from this world. The outcome is still very much undetermined."

James studied the monk, which now dangled from the Jeep's mirror and mumbled cryptically, "The future is what we make it."

17

What had Alice meant? How did attachment lead to suffering?

Ray was pondering the question, a question that had launched a religion, when he heard a familiar voice. It wasn't Alice: she was sitting silently in front of him. It had come from the woods. Ray knew that voice: it was Chase. Yet it had to be imagination, as there was no way she would be on this mountain in the dead of night.

He peered outside. A damp blanket of clouds obscured the forest. The night was oppressive, lacking even a faint breeze. Something unseen permeated the forest with a vaguely threatening presence.

Ray admonished himself: *it was ridiculous to be afraid.* He was perfectly at home in the wilderness; nature was a womb that comforted and nourished him. From the time he was a small boy, he had felt at one with the primal energy that emanated from the earth. On too many occasions to count, he had savored the exhilarating sense of oneness. But tonight the forest was not his friend, it seemed accusatory, angry.

Feeling his sanity was in peril, he realized he must focus on his concern for Chase. For a few tense minutes, he could only hear the rustle of leaves and the faint rasp of his own breathing. Then her call came from beyond the trees: "Ray, please."

Without so much as a glance at Alice, Ray scrambled out the door and sprinted toward the tree line. Underbrush snagged his pants and slowed his advance. He heard Chase call out once again and he came to a sudden halt. This time her voice came from behind him, so he doubled back. He had almost retraced his steps when she called his name one more time. But it came from another direction.

He wondered if his senses were betraying him or was someone playing tricks? His heart quickened. Was he panicking? He forced a deep breath, and listened. *Why was Chase here?* He had been gone one evening. That would not be sufficient reason to form a search party. It didn't make sense.

He was about to return to the cabin's warmth when an inner voice nagged: what if this time was different? What if she had become worried? What if, when he didn't return, she had set off looking for him? What if she was lost and frightened in these woods? Could he take the chance?

Just to be safe, he retraced his steps. He stumbled upon a fallen tree he didn't recall seeing previously. A whimper issued from behind the log. He rushed ahead, though he was barely able to see in the dark. Again, he heard a whisper of a whimper. It wasn't human; maybe a small animal.

A memory stirred: *Biscuit, his childhood pet.* Was the cocker spaniel on the other side of the log shivering with fear and cringing in a pose Ray thought he had flushed from his memory long ago? It was the pose the little dog assumed while being beaten by Ray's father. He recalled what Alice had taught: painful memories were not gone; they were merely covered up by an act of forgetting. Years ago, Ray had felt Biscuit's pain as though it were his own. *This must be some kind of memory*, he figured. It was not possible for the dog to be on the other side of the log: Biscuit had died years ago.

Ray tiptoed forward. That's when he saw a creature crawl through a patch of moonlight. The beast inched forward, fixed its yellowish eyes on its prey, prepared to lunge, and growled a warning. Ray was trained to never turn his back on a predator: do not run; control your fear; face the threat square on; make yourself as big as possible.

Ray maintained his composure—until the beast bared its fangs and signaled it was no cowering dog. It was a sick animal, perhaps a rabid wolf. As the misshapen creature crept forward, its yellow eyes casting a sickly glow, Ray became certain the beast was afflicted with evil that arose from beyond the natural order. If this was true, he surmised, the rules dictating patience were an invitation to disaster.

Ray burst into a run. The wolf beast gave pursuit. As Ray crashed through the underbrush, he realized he had never been chased, except in childhood dreams. The thought distracted him and his foot landed awkwardly on a fallen branch. The rotted wood crumbled, his ankle turned, and he pitched headfirst into the unforgiving trunk of a forty-foot pine. The impact dropped him.

The sticky warmth of the blood trickling down his forehead summoned a sense of déjà-vu. The image of a cracked windshield flashed. Ray made out the startled face of an endearing gnome with a pointy beard staring back at him from the other side of the shattered glass. The gnome's comical appearance brought a smile to Ray's lips, which the gnome misread. Assuming Ray was fine, the cheery character disappeared with a whimsical wink.

The vision had distracted Ray, giving the beast an opportunity to attack. Ray spun left. Jagged teeth narrowly missed his thigh. And then once again, he evaded the jaws that slammed shut with a wet slap. He scrambled to his feet and sprinted between the trees. He slid down a gully on slippery pine needles, jumped up, and continued his mad dash. He catapulted blindly in a new direction and slammed into a solid object. The unexpected collision staggered him. He glanced up to find a ghoulish, foul-smelling figure draped in a black, threadbare overcoat. The wolf-creature dropped at the ghoul's feet in quiet submission. This was no doubt the beast's master, Ray thought, upon seeing the same grayish complexion and yellowish eyes.

"Get your animal under control," Ray screamed. With embarrassment he realized how pathetic he sounded. This was not a friendly neighbor whose pet had roamed off leash; rather, he had encountered a malevolent force that meant him harm.

The ghoulish figure stepped into the moonlight and Ray recognized the sardonic features of his father, or what used to be his father. Questions pelted him like hail in an ice storm. *How? Why?* He had not seen nor heard from the man in years. How had the old man fallen into such an inhuman condition? How had he managed to track Ray to this mountain?

Ray's curiosity cost him. The figure—who had once been his father—sent him reeling with a backhand blow. He slammed into a tree with the back of his head and slid to the ground, staring up at his adversary with blurred vision. His fear became oddly visible and radiated into space like ripples on a pond. Before he could escape, a female figure, a wispy phantom in a white-lace wedding gown, appeared in a clearing in the dense forest.

"Chase?" Ray gasped.

She ran from him, with an enormous train of white satin billowing behind her. Though these events made no sense, none whatsoever, Ray knew he had to get up on his feet. As he stood, he nimbly sidestepped a punch. Then the ghoulish figure with the frozen sneer launched a second strike. Ray again ducked the blow and then sprinted after Chase. Before he could catch her, she disappeared behind a tree. Ray paused to catch his breath. A moment later, she reappeared, this time pushing a baby carriage, a sturdy gray affair with hard rubber tires.

Ray closed his eyes and willed his brain to process the experience. He tried forcing a veneer of logic over the top of the insanity, but the oddness persisted: *His father had morphed into a vicious creature. Chase pushed a baby carriage through the forest. If this was a bad dream, it was time to wake up.* But Ray knew he was wide awake and this was no dream. Though he had suffered painful blows, those blows had not awakened him into a different state.

Perhaps he had been drugged and was hallucinating? He longed for sobriety, he willed himself to sober up, but there was no change of scenery. He knew there was no easy escape; he must allow the altered state to run its course. All he could do, all he must do, was manage his fear.

Chase tripped on the gown, staggered and fell to her knees. The carriage caromed off a tree and rolled to a stop. The beast blocked Ray's path. Hallucination or not, he knew he must protect Chase. The carriage needed no defense, he assured himself, as he and Chase were childless. It must be a mere prop, perhaps a symbol meant to prod Ray to stop his waffling and make concrete plans. He got the message.

Off to his right, the cabin was visible. If he ran toward the safety of the structure, the creature would no doubt pursue him and leave Chase alone. But running seemed absurd. Rather, he thought, he should confront the creature and challenge it to do its worse. Perhaps it was only a phantom, he mused. If so, it must lack power beyond what he granted to it with his imagination. *After all, what did it matter if he was mutilated during a hallucination?*

He fingered the drying blood on his forehead and felt the throbbing ache in his jaw. His injuries felt real enough. He couldn't take a chance that Chase would be hurt. His only option was to run and create a diversion. He sprinted, baiting the beast. Three-quarters of the way across the clearing the soil mysteriously softened into mud. He slipped, scrambled to his feet, and slipped again. He was becoming bogged down. His legs burned with exhaustion, nonetheless, he willed them to keep churning through the slop.

At last, exhausted, he crawled onto the porch, rose to his knees, lowered his shoulder, and body-slammed the cabin door. The wood splintered, the latch gave way. He headed straight for the fireplace and armed himself with an iron poker. He spun around to face the demonic creature.

Instead, he encountered Alice, covering an amused smirk with the back of her hand.

18

Chase had finally drifted off, her head resting comfortably on the edge of Ray's bed. A noise from the hallway startled her out of her sleep. Her puffy and creased eyes settled on Randi, who entered looking well rested. Chase managed little more than a groggy grunt.

"You okay?" Randi asked.

"Yeah, sure."

"Liar."

"What a strange dream. It seemed so real. Ray could hear me, but he couldn't answer."

"I like to think he can hear us," Randi added as she brushed a stray hair from Chase's face. "It can't hurt to hope, can it?"

Chase yawned and sought to fully wake up. She studied the nurses bustling about the corridor. "Imagine being an ICU nurse. You watch patients teeter between life and death. Must be hard to deal with clueless families scared out of their minds. Like us."

Randi didn't like the direction in which the conversation was headed. She tried to set a new path. "If things were different, if you and I had met in better circumstances, we would be making small talk, gossiping about the neighbors, tiptoeing around delicate subjects, sharing family photos."

Chase smiled at Randi's tactful prying. "And we would have fretted over first impressions. I would probably be worried about advice you would give Ray. 'Stay with her, you got a good one.' Or maybe something less flattering?"

"Ray doesn't need my opinion," Randi continued. A beat later she asked wryly, "How long *have* you been dating?"

So Ray hadn't told her much. Was that a good sign, or a bad sign? "We've been together two, almost three, years. Seems longer. We made plans once. Ray was about to phone you. But then we decided to postpone the Big Day until funds for the new business were in the bank."

"That's him, always cautious. He feared fate might toss him a curve he couldn't handle." She glanced at his unmoving form. Her voice cracked, "Maybe he was right."

Chase, covering her distress, fluffed the pillow supporting Ray's head. The easy words that should offer comfort eluded her. She had to do *something*. "He always had questions," Chase said. "Questions about how things worked. Why they were the way they were. There had to be a master plan behind everything. He didn't like to think life was simply random and lacking meaning."

"I suppose I was not much help," Randi said. "I never could answer his questions about my divorce. He never understood our little domestic disaster. Guess I never really understood it either."

"Huh. Funny. He never talked about your divorce."

Randi's surprise was raw, unmasked. "Maybe I didn't

screw him up after all." A beat later, she exhaled a bitter laugh. "Who am I kidding?"

"Hey, don't even start thinking you're responsible for how someone turned out," Chase said. "Ray believed each person decides who they are. He couldn't stand the idea of being a victim. Eventually he came to the conclusion that nobody creates us, not even God."

"He lost his faith, didn't he?"

"He didn't *lose* faith, he tossed it overboard. Dropped back twenty and punted. There were too many gaping holes in the logic for his taste. He was the definition of a die-hard prag-matist. If you kicked it and it kicked back, it was real."

Randi listened, fascinated by Chase's analysis.

"We disagreed. I'd rather not think that's the way life is. I'd rather hold out for miracles." She took Ray's hand in hers.

"Me, too, dear," Randi responded. "Me, too."

Hal entered with James in tow.

Chase studied the hermit with obvious trepidation. Open-hearth cooking imbued his clothes with a smoky aroma, his beard and hair were coiffed in a woodsy style, and his ner-vous manner reminded Chase of an animal sniffing out new surroundings. She offered her hand in greeting. James shook it absently, his attention had already zeroed in on Ray. Chase flashed Hal a look—*what the hell is going on?*

Hal shrugged and watched James probe Ray's anatomy with a professional touch. When James was satisfied with his exam, he squeezed into the space at the head of the bed and cradled Ray's skull in his hands. He massaged Ray's temples with his thumbs as he hummed.

Hal shot a nervous glance at Chase and Randi. *Was that groaning or chanting?*

Chase, who had retreated to the far corner of the room, gestured impatiently to Hal. *Get your ass over here.*

Hal waved her off—*it's okay.*

James cocked his head and summoned Chase and Randi. They balked, reticent to join whatever it was he was doing. "Come, come here," he commanded in a firm voice.

"Your thoughts are very important. Grief, sadness, clinging—negative emotions impede his progress."

Chase crossed the room, flashing Hal the evil eye. *You'll pay for this.*

"Progress? His progress?" she whispered.

"James studied *The Book of the Dead*," Hal interjected.

Chase and Randi stared at Hal with slack-jawed horror.

"It prepares monks to guide departed souls as they leave this plane—"

"Oh, good, a little la la land," Chase snapped. Her meaning was clear: *Not what we need, Hal.*

Randi edged toward the door, embarking on a clandestine mission to summon the head nurse. Before she could slip out, Dr. Seidman entered. Randi's heart skipped a beat. *Be careful what you wish for,* she thought.

Seidman scanned the proceedings with a paranoid gaze.

"Sssh," Hal hissed, nodding toward James. "Ray insisted massage was the one therapy he couldn't live without."

Seidman regarded the group with skepticism reserved for alien encounters.

"No mediums, like we promised," Randi added.

Seidman mouthed "ten minutes," then spun smartly on the heels of his loafers and exited.

James followed the psychologist's departure with bemused disgust, then closed his eyes and concentrated. He placed Chase's hands on Ray's head and covered them with his own. He gestured for Randi to hold Ray's hands and motioned for Hal to touch his feet.

"He has very little attention on the body, almost none. He's lost, disoriented. He's trying to figure out what happened."

Hal studied James with bemused skepticism. Chase eyed him with raw suspicion. Randi expelled a breath, and inhaled hope for the first time since she had received the news of the accident.

James shook his head. "I don't know that he'll return. I wish I understood more… On a few occasions I've been able to establish communication. For very short periods."

For the next five minutes, the room was silent except for the low hum of James' chant.

Hal was unfazed, figuring they had nothing to lose by letting James stay. At the very least, he had done *something*. No one should criticize him for acting human in his desperate, perhaps futile, attempt to manage his fear. In the coming weeks, he might look back on this moment with embarrassment, but for now he believed he was acting in Ray's best interest.

Before another five minutes had passed, Dr. Seidman reappeared. With a brusque gesture, he signaled the end of their "séance." His thinly veiled disgust telegraphed his belief that they were engaged in tomfoolery that had no place in *his* hospital.

James stopped humming and focused his attention on Seidman. He maintained his chilled-out hermit expression, but Hal knew James tracked the psychologist's bad vibes with laser intensity. In a surprise move, James suddenly deescalated the standoff and ushered the entire group, including Seidman, out of the room.

"Let's give Ray some peace and quiet. Where can we purchase a spot of tea?"

Everyone started filing down the hall—except for Seidman. James turned on him. "You're invited. Are you coming?"

The psychologist was not accustomed to being ordered about in this setting where *he* issued the orders. He resented James' effort to take control, but, fortunately, he was too surprised and off balance to protest further.

At that moment, Hal knew he had been right to summon James. The hermit's isolation had not blunted his people skills; his solitude had paradoxically fine-tuned his ability to track human emotions. And, at this moment, Hal could tell James was tracking Seidman's negative thoughts as if they were psychic land mines.

In the cafeteria, the guest from the mountain charmed the help into locating green tea, although it ended up being the chilled-and-bottled variety, not the traditional bag designed for brewing.

Chase turned an emotional corner and now found herself pleased with James' visit. He may have looked like a bear coming out of hibernation, but he obviously possessed enough worldly charm to smooth over tense circumstances.

She wondered if the hermit hid his true nature on purpose or out of neglect.

Once settled at a table, Seidman pressed James, "Sir, what's your line of work?"

"Pediatrics," James replied.

Was this peculiar man mocking him? Seidman's skepticism raged.

"I was a practicing physician for years until I realized something was missing."

Seidman, taken off guard, rolled back his hostility. Perhaps the scruffy beard and unorthodox manner hid something substantial. It wouldn't be the first time an M.D. had gone off the rails, overwhelmed by stress. Or perhaps an ethical dilemma had driven him out of the profession.

"We fail to treat the whole patient," James continued. "We medicate symptoms and ignore underlying causes. I sold my practice. Traveled. Spent time in the Orient. Became conversant with alternative treatment modalities."

"Holistic medicine," Seidman said with slight displeasure. He was beginning get the full picture, and it did not lessen his disdain. In his mind, doctors that abandoned science-based medicine to embrace quackery were even more offensive than those who did not know better. "You no longer practice?"

"Decided to take a few years off. Followed the edict 'heal thyself, physician.'"

"And how's that going?" Randi asked.

"I'm pleased. I anticipate opening a new practice within a year or maybe two."

"You'll return to treating children?" Chase asked.

An enigmatic grin formed, "Given that we're all children, I guess you could say that."

Seidman's cheeks glowed pink with irritation. James' uncouth appearance, his unorthodox views, and the blasé manner in which he approached life—everything about James irritated him. But, before he could mount an offensive, Chase's sister Eva arrived with Bryce in tow.

Chase hugged the new arrivals. "Eva, I'm so glad you came. Everyone, this is my sister, Eva. And her daughter, Bren."

Eva squeezed Chase's hand in a silent gesture of sympathy. Bren, a free spirit unshackled by conventional constraints, remained oblivious to the gravity of the situation. She had not yet been fitted for tact's straitjacket. She took one look at James and stuck out her tongue.

To Seidman's horror and to Hal's delight, James mirrored her gesture with a goofy face.

Bren put her hands on her hips in a show of mock outrage.

James hid his face in his hands as if he was unspeakably abashed.

Bren giggled and traded a high five with him, followed by a low five. In less than a minute, James had made a new friend and had embarrassed Seidman, who quickly realized that this strange man was not merely a pediatrician, but a doctor with a remarkable bedside manner, a master at establishing rapport with young patients.

Eva, sporting an apologetic smile, stepped in and wrapped her arms around Bren, regaining control. "How's Ray doing?" she asked.

Siedman challenged James. "You're the medical doctor here, what's *your* prognosis?"

James ignored the covert hostility. "I'm here as a friend of the family. And, as a friend, and not the attending physician, I recommend we visit the accident scene."

He expected enthusiasm. He received blank stares.

"In order to discern exactly what happened to Ray, so we can diagnose his condition, we should start at the beginning," he explained.

Bren's young voice cut the silence, "What happened to Uncle Ray? What's wrong with him?"

They all stared at her, thinking the same thing: *how do you explain impending death to an eight-year-old?*

19

"Quit laughing," Ray exclaimed. "Quit with your silly games. My fiancé—she's out there being attacked by a rabid animal."

Alice's laughter died down but she continued to smile as she pointed behind Ray. He turned, prepared to confront the beast. Instead, he faced a scruffy, trembling dog, hardly the rabid beast that had pursued him. Looking closer, Ray recognized it was Biscuit, the precocious cocker spaniel adopted when Ray was ten, the tumultuous year before his parents' divorce.

"Biscuit? Is that you, boy?"

The small dog shied away. He was hurt, or at the very least cold and lost. Ray tried to get a grip on his crazy emotions. Biscuit died years ago. And yet there before him was a cocker spaniel, shivering and cringing with fear. Had he managed to bring to life a painful memory locked away in the dungeon of his mind for decades? But how was that possible? His life, which had taken on the quality of a strange dream, was careening out of control.

Ray was consumed with pity at the sight of the cowering little dog baring his teeth in anticipation of being struck.

"Relax, Biscuit. I won't hurt you." But as Ray leaned down, Biscuit looked up with jaundiced, bloodshot eyeballs. Foamy saliva streaked with blood dripped from his jowls. Flea-infested hair bristled on his back. He curled his thin lips and exposed glistening wet canines.

Ray took his eyes off the macabre sight when an unexpected clatter arose from beyond the tree line. It was a sound he knew well—a rock climber's backpack stuffed with pitons and carabiners knocked against a granite wall. Ray scanned the horizon—there was no sign of the ghoul or of Chase. Then he heard a faint and distant call for help that sounded like… It was Hal's voice. Ray sprinted through the woods toward the distressed voice.

He stumbled upon a steep ravine that blocked his path. Though a heavy mist hindered his vision, he could make out Hal, on the other side of the ravine, dangling at the end of a blue nylon rope. His left arm hung limp, dislocated, the humorous bone separated from the shoulder socket. His right knee jutted out at a stomach-churning angle. Blood oozed from a gash in his scalp into his sandy hair. His distressed features telegraphed "save me." And yet Hal yelled out: "Let me go. Save yourself."

Save him? Or let him go? Ray could not depend upon Hal's judgment, as his injuries must have rendered him delirious. Though a rescue attempt would be an invitation to death, Hal *was* his best friend—*Ray had no choice.*

He inched down the rocky face of the ravine, until he encountered an eight-foot sheer drop. He failed to find a detour around the drop. He faced the granite wall and lowered himself down the rock face, his climber's grip supporting his weight. With his toes he tapped the rock, searching for a foothold.

Finally, he spotted a small shelf worn into the rock two feet to his right and six feet below. Before he could lower his feet into the alcove, he was stopped cold—the warning rattle was unmistakable. The coiled snake on the shelf was barely visible, but within striking distance. The viper hammered its venom into Ray's calf.

Cursing and kicking, Ray muscled himself up onto the ledge and inspected the bite saturated with poison. It swelled rapidly. He glanced across the ravine at Hal who was resigned to his fate. For Ray, it was a bitter defeat. First, Chase. Now, he had failed Hal. He bent over and vomited.

Chase's voice echoed off the rocks. "Ray, it's going to be okay."

He looked up to find her standing over him with a sympathetic smile. But it was not Chase, it was Alice.

"Your friends will be okay," she said. "But you have much to learn and time is running out."

She had to be joking. Chase was lost in the forest pushing a baby carriage. His father was stalking him. His best friend was injured and stranded across the ravine at the end of a rope. And he was dying from a venomous snakebite. And she wanted to...

"Stop!" he screamed. "No more lessons. I've been bitten. I don't know—"

"I know you don't know!" Alice snapped, as if admonishing a schoolboy. "Think, Ray, think. The mind: mental energy images. They stay with the soul after it departs the body."

Ray trembled. The pain in his leg throbbed. "What does that have to do with me?"

"A soul remains entangled in the mental energy forms of its former body."

She held up her arm—and it disappeared down to her elbow.

Shock stampeded Ray out of his pain-induced stupor. *Alice was dead!* He was face to face with a disembodied spirit, a ghost. No wonder he couldn't figure her out, and no wonder she didn't seem to care about his present condition.

She read his horror and said, "The departed soul lives in an idealistic world of thought forms." Her entire arm disappeared, and then reappeared. She pointed to Ray's hand, "Look."

He looked down to find his hand fading and disappearing. Alice's words came back to him: *A soul that has left the body remains entangled in mental energy copies of its former body. It may believe it still possesses its body, as the soul will mistake the mental energy for the real thing.*

Nausea flooded Ray's consciousness. This wasn't a mere hallucination. He hadn't bumped his head. He wasn't dreaming. HE WAS DEAD.

His "world" shattered into a thousand chaotic pieces: Pictures. Memories. Thoughts. The equivalent of twenty television signals simultaneously pummeled his awareness.

In the midst of the chaos, Alice's face appeared, steady and loving. An act of pure will and pure intention placed her image in his disembodied mind. Her compassionate face was an inviting icon in a sea of disturbing images. Her presence was the only stable reality to which he could cling.

"Do you understand now?" she asked.

Yes. Ray understood and he was grief stricken. He would never hold Chase again. He would never again joke with Hal. His plans for the future had been cancelled. His hopes, dreams and grand ideas had come to nothing. Everything he assumed he knew about reality had been turned upside down. His fear, anger, and pain dissipated into a yawning, bottomless void.

He remembered Alice telling him that attachment causes suffering. And there was no doubt that he was strongly attached to his body, his work, his ideas, and to the people in his life. Now they had been taken from him. He suffered. He was dead.

20

Hal's Jeep wound through the pass, its snow tires, armed with porcelain studs, gripped the ice as he navigated switchbacks. James rode shotgun. Chase rode in back, taking in the scenery: bluish-green pines silhouetted against blazing white snow and rich azure skies. Though the cold mountain air chafed her fair complexion, she mused that *it felt good to be alive.* The thought unleashed a flood of guilt—feeling alive was something Ray could no longer share. He might never regain consciousness. *Could she live with that?*

Hal executed a controlled skid off the main road and bumped down a seldom-used mining road, plowing through foot-high drifts for a quarter mile. He parked downhill from the damaged pine that had broken the Explorer's fall.

They hopped out and scaled the steep hillside. Hal kept a steady hand on Chase's back to prevent her from falling but she took to the grade with the nonchalance of a mountain goat. She did not lose her footing until she slid to a stop near the wounded tree.

"You okay?" Hal asked, thinking perhaps she had slipped on a patch of ice.

Chase rested with her hands on her knees and her eyes closed. She gestured toward the tree. She had not been overwhelmed by the steep grade, but rather by raw emotion. The sight of the mangled tree trunk, severed branches, shattered glass, and fluttering police tape had shaken her composure. Before Hal could offer comforting words, she whipped out her cellphone.

"How are you doing, Mom?" Chase said. "Is he doing any better?"

Chase, for the first time, had felt comfortable calling Randi "Mom." Viewing the site where both their lives had taken a horrific turn made her feel closer than ever to Randi, who would soon be her child's grandmother. They were now family, even though Randi did not yet know how strongly intertwined their lives had become.

"We're okay," Chase went on. "It's really cold up here. Pretty, but not real friendly." That was an understatement; the site was unforgiving. *All the wishes and prayers in the world would not make a dent in this pile of rocks*, Chase reckoned. "Well, let us know if anything changes… Call us if we need to get back, okay? Bye."

She looked up to find Hal, with his six-foot-four reach, leaning over the police tape and hanging the toy monk on a broken branch. James directed the "tree trimming."

"Up. Up. Move it to the left. Right there. Perfect."

"Is there a reason for this…?" Chase asked. "Did we come up here to solve the mystery behind the accident? Or to decorate a tree?"

James was unfazed. "Buddhist and Christian teachings tell

us that life continues after death. Death is not the end of the road."

Chase allowed her stress to do the talking. "Ray isn't dead, unless you know something I don't."

"He's not dead, but those who come near to death often return with stories of a life beyond this one. They describe moving through transitions or stages. They claim they've learned the essential qualities of life: love, compassion, and wisdom."

"What are you saying?"

"At first Ray may not know the truth regarding his condition. Eventually, however, it will dawn on him that he is no longer among the living."

"Nearly dead," Chase said.

"Though we may not see him, he may... access our thoughts."

"Right. I wouldn't know. Are we supposed to do something?"

James knew these ideas were not easy to grasp. "When he tries to sort out what happened, his attention may fix on this crash site. All we can do is be here and allow our presence to serve as a beacon. We must clear our minds."

Chase had assumed they were visiting the accident scene to unravel a medical mystery. She had expected they would determine the speed at which Ray skidded off the road, the angle of the collision with the tree, and the position of the vehicle when it came to a stop. She had expected they would engage in a crime scene investigation. Instead, James had taken off on a bizarre tangent.

"What? What's the matter?" James queried.

"I've never cleared my mind," she said, fumbling for a way to opt out. "I'm not certain I can. Tell someone not to think of a pink elephant and the next thing you know, they can't think of anything *but* a pink elephant."

"Good. Think of a pink elephant or don't think of a pink elephant. Either will be fine."

Hal was puzzled at Chase's brusque response to James. It wasn't like her. "Chase, you and Ray had a ritual for ridding yourselves of the day's distractions, for quieting the noise. He told me—"

"I'll try."

"There are stages of dying," James lectured. "At first the deceased does not recognize his condition. He wanders in confusion, tossed about in a world of images. Symbolic visions and hallucinations appear. If he is wise, he might realize that his thoughts create his world."

"So the world is an illusion?" Hal was amused by James' idealism.

"Something along those lines," James responded. "At some point he may see happy visions. And then he'll experience terrifying visions. He must come to recognize his own fears."

"And then—"

"He may think of death as a flame passing from wick to wick. His future may stretch out in front of him without end. But he may also undergo frightening and challenging trials. Eventually, he must recognize that his fears are the products of his own mind. This is not as easy as it sounds. The manner in which he completes his lessons will determine…"

"If he will return?" Chase asked.

"Some visit the other side and return," James replied.

"You really know how this stuff works?" Hal asked.

"I'm not a master. But I know the principles. Over thousands of years, much of the information has become altered or lost. It's difficult to find the pure lessons. So one has to cobble together pieces, as one finds them."

Chase interjected, "How can monks know this stuff unless they died?"

"There's not a one of us that has not died many, many times," James replied. "We do not remember. So how do I know? Monastics who have spent their entire life perfecting their awareness have provided descriptions of the afterlife. These monks have learned to pass from one conscious state to another. And when they master the intermediate stage, they tend to become more lucid. They see an enlarged view of reality."

Chase toyed with a thought: "So these guys should still be around, somewhere. Right?"

"Yeah?"

"You said the lessons were altered. Maybe it's time for a fresh edition."

James, retaining his professorial demeanor, nodded approvingly. "You catch on quickly. Monastics are constantly clearing the path and sharing the wisdom with others. A new edition is constantly unfolding. But their work is not well known."

"Figures," Chase said. "As soon as you get lost, the map is nowhere to be found. When Ray returns, maybe he'll bring home a decent map."

"Let's be still," James said, gesturing for quiet. "Maybe our presence will be a sign he will recognize."

21

"You cannot stay forever," Alice said. "Not on this mountain, not in this cabin. You will grow tired of such a small world. Besides, it isn't allowed."

"Where should I go?" Ray inquired. He no longer resented her. She was his life raft.

"The decision is yours. But we must hurry. Are you ready to continue?"

"I have a choice?" He hoped there was a way to turn back the clock.

"One always has a choice," Alice said.

Ray had not said a word, yet she knew exactly what he was thinking. They were communicating telepathically. *Why not? He was dead.* He recalled how his hand had disappeared, and how he had realized the body he now possessed was nothing more than a glorified phantasm. It was a heavenly body, a glorified body. It was a mental construct.

A terrifying thought struck: *What if this phantom body disappeared as well?* What if it faded like the emulsion on aging film stock? That would leave him with… absolutely nothing. If the physical body dissipated, dust-to-dust, and the mental body was but a chimera, what was left? Once again, he came face to face with the unsettling idea of No Thing.

"I'm not sure I understand… How thought works."

He had not spoken aloud. He was sharing his thoughts with Alice, not words. For the first time, he became aware of the blazing speed of telepathic dialogue; he had to work to keep up.

"Let us review. I'll try to be clear. The transition from nothing to something is as simple as a thought," she said, clicking her fingers. "When you perceive, you see thought forms. When you see me, you're looking at a thought form."

She disappeared, reappeared next to the fireplace, disappeared again and then reappeared by the door.

"Now, you try. Get the idea of a balloon. Place it out here."

Ray, expecting failure, shrugged his shoulders and imagined a red balloon floating above the table. It took over a minute, but he managed to conjure a small, wobbly, purple balloon near the ceiling.

"But is it *real?*" He turned to Alice and the balloon instantly disappeared.

"That's a mental creation, a thought form. You project a thought and perceive that thought. You are a No Thing that creates thought forms."

She sketched an illustration. It lifted off the screen she had used previously and floated in mid-air. "You were accustomed to looking at images on a screen. That fit within your sense of reality. Now you know you've only been viewing my thoughts, so we no longer need the screen."

She created a sphere and then a second. She pointed to the

first sphere. "Imagine your awareness being fully contained in this balloon. Consider that is your personal universe, the universe of your awareness, which contracts or expands in response to your will."

She turned to the second sphere. "This is my personal universe in which I don't perceive what you perceive. When we exist solely in our personal universes, we exist separately."

Alice's spheres or balloons, representing symbolic personal universes, floated toward one another and partially overlapped. "Where the spheres overlap, a part of your universe exists in common with a part of my universe. We might say that we share the space in that overlapping region. In that shared space, we can share forms."

In the overlapping region of space, an image of a cabin appeared, a miniature version of the structure they occupied.

"In shared space we see each other's thoughts. This ability to share takes shape and becomes real the moment we agree to create in unison."

"I don't remember agreeing… not to anything like that."

"True, you don't remember basic agreements. Hardly anyone does. They took place so very long ago. At the moment souls emerged into existence they entered into an agreement. The act of sharing space was simultaneous with the moment of entering into existence. When we entered creation's shared space, we automatically entered into agreement with others. It was instantaneous."

"How's that?

"Some call this type of being together 'mystical unity.' Or they might call it 'communion with God.' This supernatural sharing of a common space and common being-thought-forms is spiritual unity or communion. We might say that spiritual consciousness emerged from divine consciousness. With spiritual consciousness we have the ability to re-enter into the mystical unity we call divine love. Existing in a state of divine agreement, in divine relationship, is as close as one individual can come to another. It consists of fully overlapping awareness. We know it as being in unity."

"I seem to have forgotten."

"There's a reason you forgot. The original agreements became automatic, something we no longer had to think about. Once souls went on 'automatic pilot' they became forgetful. Souls even forgot their own spiritual nature. They forgot who they were, where they were, or how they came to be there. They became lost."

Ray could not argue with her assessment. He was truly lost. Perhaps he always had been. Maybe he was what they call a "lost soul." He looked around at the cabin. He didn't remember how he came to be there. He did not remember how he had died—let alone how he had arrived in this universe.

He recalled the terror he had felt in the woods… "That man… My father. Was he really in this world? When he struck… I felt it. He was here, right?"

"Yes, he was. His sickness repulsed you. It made you afraid. In this stage of your spiritual journey, fear is easily summoned."

"It's not all angels and peace and love, is it?"

"On this side, beyond mortal life, you will see many faces.

It's easy to become confused. Fear overwhelms judgment. But, if I'm not mistaken, you were hounded by an even greater fear than your father."

Ray pictured the wolf's yellow eyes and disease-ridden body.

"I did not fear the creature more than his master."

"I meant your fear of losing someone close to you. Losing love."

"Chase?"

He didn't want to think about Chase. He didn't want to contemplate the future that had been brutally ripped away, canceled. He didn't want the burden of regret. But regret nonetheless rose like an inexorable tide. He had caused the delay. He had delayed the marriage—his incessant craving for worldly security had caused him to balk, time after time. He wondered if the baby carriage represented missed opportunities and unrealized dreams.

He turned to Alice, "Was the baby carriage a symbolic message?"

He thought he saw her features soften with compassion, but she said, or thought, nothing to comfort him. Instead she went on with the lesson.

"Let us continue…" A dozen spheres popped into view. They overlapped in one small region, which glowed. "Any number of individuals can participate in a common agreement: hundreds, thousands, millions, or more. That is what these spheres or balloons represent. There's no limit to the number of souls, all emerging from divine consciousness, that can enter into agreement and out of chaos give shape to patterns. The forms that are created are simply a multitude of agreements."

"The laws of physics emerge from supernatural agreement?" Ray queried with a thought. He had started to grasp the concept, though it was terribly elusive.

"Discovering the laws of physics is one way to discover the agreements. When we study forms, we begin to understand the created patterns, and those shapes are agreements that we call laws of nature."

"Collaborative creation?"

"After we investigate the supernatural origin of the universe, we understand why all souls perceive the same forms and patterns. It is the power of supernatural agreement."

"Like existing in the Mind of God," offered Ray.

"Individual minds in unity with the Mind of God. Good way to put it," she said.

"So this is a great deal more than our ordinary idea of agreement. It is like some kind of co-being."

"Yes. It's the result of being-thought-forms arising out of the unity of spiritual consciousness and divine consciousness."

"Thought forms that we all share," he thought, syncing his epiphany with his telepathic communication with Alice.

He recalled Professor Kidner's words, but it was Alice who finished his thought: "This is what your professor meant when he said the world is an illusion. It's a way of saying that creation does not exist separate from thought. This also appears in the Gospel of John."

Alice's collection of spheres disappeared and was replaced

by three partially overlapping spheres. In one, a purple sphere appeared; in another, a red cube; in yet another, a yellow pyramid. The region of their overlap remained empty.

Ray understood Alice's meaning: three spirits each created a thought form in their own universe, a thought form not perceived by the others. Then she moved the sphere, the cube, and the pyramid together into the overlapping region.

Again, Ray understood that when thought forms appeared in the shared space, with shared energy and matter, they became part of what people mistakenly called the objective world. Actually, it was subjective, from top to bottom.

She referenced the common region. "This shared space represents our common universe. The universe we share."

"Why does it exist? What's its purpose?"

"It's a place for us to come together to play a game."

"A game? Now you've lost me. Or you're joking around when we do not have time for such humor."

"Think about it. If you want to play baseball with friends, you must all be on the same field, you must agree on the rules, you must use a ball that all can see. When do we have the most fun? When we're playing, right?"

"Life is not always a game."

"Life is *always* a game. At times we may be unable or unwilling to play. We may sit out. We may fail to even recognize that we're in a game. That's when life no longer seems like play. It's not so much fun when we quit playing but we still must suit up and get out on the field."

She waved her hand. The spheres collapsed into one—a small sphere glowing so bright it was nearly impossible to behold. In an instant, it expanded like the Big Bang.

"Can I share a story with you?"

"As long as it does not make me late for wherever I must be."

"It's an epic story, but will not take me long."

Ray nodded, finding it odd being told a story telepathically.

"Once upon a time, the shared universe became very desirable. Souls fixated on forms. They loved the forms. They were extremely desirable. And then the souls lost sight of their spiritual essence. Soon forms became more valuable than souls, more valuable than love. Eventually, souls had become total prisoners of their desire. Attached to forms, desiring forms, they even forgot they were immortal souls. They thought, 'I'm this object or that object.' They became hopelessly entangled in forms."

"Entangled?"

"When forms became more valuable than the creators of forms, this desire for forms brought about a sticky attachment. But there was a problem—"

"Things did not go well." Ray anticipated the next story beat.

Alice continued, "Because the forms were created in unison with God and other souls, they were not the property of any one individual. They were shared possessions and thus they could be taken away—and that loss brings about suffering."

"The price to be paid for desire and attachment," Ray acknowledged.

"In our personal universe, we own our creations outright. They are ours alone. When we share with others, however, we do not totally control the forms, so we may experience loss."

"That explains mankind's eternal struggle over possessions," Ray sighed.

"In our own minds, we create forms or images as we wish. With shared forms, we're not totally in charge. We may not like the result of our interaction with others. We may cease to fully own our 'dreams.' And thus we may experience displeasure when sharing brings about imperfections. This displeasure becomes especially acute if we fail to admire the creations of others."

Ray sensed an important lesson in the phrase *if we fail to admire the thought creations of others*. He was beginning to understand that when we refuse to admire the thoughts of others, we also diminish reality for that person. He began to imagine that life was a constant battle over whose vision would be accepted as reality. It was often a matter of whose views would dominate.

Alice continued, "Material forms may be hoarded, which creates the illusion of scarcity. This leads to jealousy and envy. Suffering arises when souls overlook the ever-present potential for abundance. Scarcity is an artificial condition."

While her lessons were new to Ray, the knowledge she imparted was ancient, a river of truth that flowed through eternity. For a fraction of a second, Ray floated on that current.

"What about God?" he asked.

"If God is Creator and we are created *in his image*, then we possess, to some degree, his ability to create as well."

This was not only a new concept for Ray but also one that startled him. Some people imagined God creating humanoids as flesh bodies. If one understood biology, this made little sense. The manner in which new bodies were created was well established. The "God as puppeteer" idea did not inspire Ray; he had little patience for such flawed concepts. But this was different. The idea that a Creator endowed souls as creators in his own image—that was an idea he could entertain.

Ray's attention fixed on another concept that had always bothered him. "Some people say we are all One. They argue that upon death our individuality dissolves into a cosmic sea of energy."

"And yet here we are. You can see that I'm not you and you're not me," Alice projected.

Ray had to admit she was right. Here he was on "the other side" and clearly he had not dissolved into oneness. He had not dissolved into an ocean of energy. Though his conditions had changed profoundly, he still enjoyed a continuity of consciousness. He was conscious as Ray, if not in bodily form. "If we're individual souls, then where does the idea of monism come from?"

This time she did not feed him an answer. "It's time you started thinking," she said.

Ray began to reflect on the riddle: If we're not part of a cosmic energy soup—what makes some people think we are? He projected multiple spheres into space, representing the awareness of multiple spirits. He collapsed the spheres into one common sphere—the physical universe. At that moment, the answer came to him. The shared focus on a common space with common energy forms made it seem "all one." The error was taking up a compulsive focus on the material universe.

"We forget that we are immortal souls and we identify with the material world, with matter and energy. This leads us to identify with all energy and matter. This leads to the belief that we act in a manner consistent with material properties, rather than knowing our immaterial properties."

"Right." Alice projected an hourglass. She vanished the top half, leaving only the pinched neck and the bottom. "Before individual souls tumble into shared physical space they're free of matter energy constraints. Think of the hourglass neck as a portal into this universe. Metaphorically, individuals enter through the portal."

Like Alice falling into the rabbit hole, Ray thought.

Alice continued. "In the bottom half of the hourglass, we occupy space with other souls. As we fall into agreement our thoughts become synchronized."

"But we're still individuals," Ray noted.

"That's easy to demonstrate. You are you. And I am, Alice. We are not one, not identical. The claim 'we are all one' conflates sharing a common universe with being one overall individual."

"I get it," Ray said. "An audience views a film in unison, but they do not become one observer. They have a common experience and then walk out of the theater as individuals."

Alice continued projecting her thoughts.

"When we achieve a state of mystical unity, we experience a type of at-one-ness. This can be a very powerful experience of divine love. Once we have a taste of that experience, we are constantly seeking to repeat it. The experience of divine love and a shared at-one-ness is the most valued state of being possible. This is the goal of all mystics."

Suddenly, Ray experienced something totally unexpected and quite odd: he found himself inside a blue sphere, not unlike a large blue balloon. Though he could not see Alice, he could feel her presence.

She had become at-one-with his mind; her mind permeated his consciousness. She issued a mental command: *Grow small.* The balloon walls contracted in a series of stutter steps that he struggled to follow. *Grow large.* He synchronized his thoughts with hers as the balloon expanded. *Grow small.* It seemed he was in control of the balloon, though he also sensed she exercised control. They enjoyed perfect synchronicity. The exercise was exhilarating.

The balloon vanished. Alice sat on the edge of the table, the folds of her blue dress gathered about her knees.

"Were we one?" she asked.

"In a way."

"Were we *really* one?" she pressed.

"No, we *acted* as one."

"Correct."

"As *if* we were one."

"Right. *As if.* We could occupy the same space and see the same objects from the same point of view. *As if* we were one. We could know exactly and precisely what the other was being, doing, creating. We experienced a closeness that—"

"Is love," Ray interjected.

"The love mystics experience. As immaterial spirit, we can pervade the space of any object, be it a balloon or a flower. We can imagine ourselves to be that balloon or that flower. We can pretend or imagine ourselves to 'be' any object, any thought form."

"But then we forget what we're doing and assume that we *really are* the balloon or the flower or some other object," he added.

"Right. We can pervade the space of any object and identify with the object. We can 'be' the balloon or the flower. We can know it fully. The mistake is thinking we really *are* that object. If we make that mistake, we become attached and take on the identity of a form. And then we suffer because all forms are transitory and temporary, unlike an immortal soul."

"The object is limited, merely a created thought form," Ray added.

"We make the mistake of identifying with temporal and fleeting thought forms." She illustrated a body and a sphere of awareness. The sphere melted into the body and disappeared. "A spirit may identify with the body and think 'I am the body.'"

Ray recalled that his attachment to his body had been so overwhelming that it had negated his spiritual self-awareness. He had forgotten his true nature—even after he had arrived at his present state, near to death, beyond his current life.

"We are never truly the form," she continued. "We're immaterial spirits."

Ray recalled how attached he had been to the mental image copy of his body. He walked around in this realm as if he was still embodied. But then, when his hand had disappeared, he knew terror like never before. However, even now, while he grasped the concept intellectually, the reality in this post-mortem state was daunting.

Another question nipped at Ray's awareness. *Spirit is energy, isn't it? Wasn't that what most believed?*

"A misconception," Alice said. "Energy is a physical property. To say spirit is energy is to say spirit is physical."

The blue balloon encompassed Ray. Alice issued commands: "Pull the surface of the balloon toward you, now push it out, away from you. Were you the energy or did you expend the mental energy?"

Ray pushed the balloon away with his mind and then pulled it back in.

"You see, you're not energy, you create energy or expend energy," she said. "Identifying spirit with energy is the same as identifying spirit with matter. Spirit is neither energy nor matter. It transcends both."

Ray, in day-to-day life, had become so accustomed to speaking in terms of the properties of matter that he rarely spoke of immaterial conditions. He now realized that spirit is real even though it lacks the quality of thingness. This idea was mind-blowingly difficult: *how could something exist but not be a thing?*

Ray was beginning to understand the differences: Nothing

and Something; Creator and Created; Material and Immaterial; Spirit and Flesh. He could see how identifying with physical forms led to attachment. If a soul thoroughly believed it was the flesh body, it would not recognize its true nature. The trap was subtle and yet, at the same time, so powerful that it could blot out a soul's memory.

"You now know that in this world, in this forest and cabin, you have been clinging to a mental body that resembles your prior flesh body," she continued. "Initially, you were confused because, in life, your mind had become thoroughly entangled with the flesh body."

Ray's attention snapped to his "ghost" body. It was a mental energy copy of the body everyone knew as Ray Carte. Though he had soared to a new understanding, he could not maintain the altitude. He felt the enormous gravity of earthly life. In spite of all that he had learned, he was unable to remain detached. Instead, he felt himself sinking into an abyss.

"You must untie the knots of attachment that bind you, one by one. You must shine light into the darkness to view the chains that dictate your fate."

"These lessons—"

"Helped you glimpse the big picture. Helped you separate your mind from confusion."

"You've shown me—"

"What lies ahead."

"I no longer have a life—"

"You assume your condition is irreversible. That was not my assessment, it was yours."

"Wait. You mean being here—"

"Think back. You learned that your thoughts contribute to your future."

"I also learned that my body…" My body. It dawned on him—he did not know the condition of his body. There had been an impact. He had separated from his body. He had assumed…

"You did not look," she said. "You did not want to see. You were afraid."

Panic tightened its grip on Ray.

Alice shape-shifted into a monk sitting cross-legged before the fireplace; she had become a slightly rotund figure with a kind yet enigmatic smile. "Who am I? I'm only a simple monk. But long ago you made me promise I would help you, if you ever became lost. You insisted. You wanted me to keep you awake. You made me promise to remind you of your true nature as an immortal spirit. You forced me to enter into a vow to keep that promise. That promise has been kept."

"I don't recall."

"That's why you made me promise. You knew you were capable of forgetting. That's valuable, sometimes." The sarcasm was direct, unveiled. "Emptying your mind can also be of value."

Ray fell silent. Even his thoughts subsided. Maybe he had forgotten… the promise. He had forgotten his prayerful vow, his desire to never lose himself and fall into sleep. He had vowed to never forget who he really was—

"Our time is nearly at an end. You have a decision to make," said the monk that now morphed into a grinning Cheshire cat. "Let us bring your confusion to a conclusion."

22

Randi squeezed Ray's unfeeling fingers. Her eyes were closed; her brow was furrowed in intense prayer as if she were trying to jumpstart his body. Without pause, she had held that pose for the past hour. Father McCarty arrived and studied Ray quietly. He gently cleared his throat.

Randi startled. Her fists curled, she was prepared to battle anyone who might show up to "pull the plug." When she recognized the priest, she relaxed her defenses.

"You okay?" he asked.

She nodded but then, as if to negate her claim, Dr. Seidman walked in.

"I'll stay with her," Father McCarty quickly interjected.

"I'll be fine," Randi assured Seidman, hoping to dismiss him without being rude.

Seidman did not argue but he also did not leave. Instead, he hovered.

As Randi reached for a Kleenex she accidentally toppled her purse and spilled its contents.

Father McCarty knelt to retrieve the fallen items. He discovered a worn copy of *Alice's Adventures in Wonderland*.

He opened the tattered cover and flipped through a series of strikingly beautiful color illustrations.

"It was Ray's favorite," Randi said.

Seeing her tears, Father McCarty laid a gentle hand on her arm.

"When the call came with news of Ray's accident, I booked a flight. While I waited for the cab, I rummaged through things Ray left behind many years ago. I found that lovely little book. When he was young I would read to him. He would ask, over and over, to hear the story of Alice."

McCarty handed her the book. For a moment, it appeared she was going to read to Ray, as if she was in his boyhood bedroom. It seemed that she imagined she was going to read to a sleepy child, rather than a grown man in a coma.

When Seidman resumed his pacing, McCarty couldn't tell if the psychologist was confused or angry. He pretended the nervous pacing didn't bother him, but he secretly wondered whether the man didn't have more productive things to do with his time.

Sensing that Randi felt a similar discomfort, he broke the silence. "Dear, if it would help, read to him. No one objects."

She dabbed a tear with her sleeve, but otherwise remained still. She stared at the book as if it were the most precious object in the world. Father McCarty, who had seen too many moments just like this one, recited a silent prayer.

* * *

Ray followed the Cheshire cat. They levitated and rose above the cabin with phantoms surrounding them on all sides. The ethereal creatures beckoned to Ray with promises of bliss. Wispy tendrils stroked his hair and face, lulling him toward slumber. Ray did not feel comforted; rather, he sensed profound danger. He knew that Alice was not playing games. This was no test. He had to be strong and stay awake.

The phantoms peeled away one by one, only to be replaced by an alluring apparition. In the far distance a magnificent glow beckoned with aesthetic rainbow hues. Alice's telepathic voice, which issued from the Cheshire cat, delivered a warning: he must remain focused and could not succumb to any temptation.

The heavenly beauty of the dancing light was hard to resist; nonetheless, Ray hardened his will and fixed on the Cheshire cat with renewed determination.

* * *

On the mountain, the wind subsided. The monk icon, hanging from the tree branch, became perfectly still.

Hal and Chase looked on as James circled the crash site, meditating. For nearly thirty minutes they had been silent, each lost in their own thoughts. Their prayer-like tranquility was shattered when a bobcat streaked across the snowy landscape toward them. The wild cat appeared headed straight for the damaged tree. Once it drew near it slowed and inched forward in a predator's crouch.

Hal's instincts kicked in. He drew himself up tall, but remained still. Wild cats were common on the front range of the mountains, but they usually avoided human contact. As far as Hal knew, no bobcat had ever attacked a group of people. Yet something drew this cat in their direction.

The crouching animal fixed its hunter's stare, exploded into a sprint, and tore up the tree. Its sharp claws shredded bark as it ascended. Crawling out on a branch, the cat reached down and batted the monk with its paw.

Hal traded smiles with Chase. They studied the odd but beautiful feline, awed by its bold playfulness.

James, eyes closed, continued pacing the snowy ground in a meditative reverie. He saw nothing of the cat. Instead, he was a spectator in a supernatural theater. He viewed Ray's ghostly image peering back at him through the shattered windshield of an Explorer SUV.

* * *

Ray glanced at the image of his body crumpled behind the steering wheel. Blood trickled down the forehead. He knew intuitively that he viewed a previously blocked memory. As he settled down into the image of the broken body, he peered out the windshield. The scene that had once been veiled by unconsciousness began to take shape.

He revisited the moment of impact, the instant he had found himself outside his body. In that instant amnesia had taken over and nullified his memory. Now, revisiting that moment, he felt no pain, only remorse. The act of inspecting the damaged body was difficult. He did not want to know its pain. Besides, he was now outside the mortal shell. He was FREE.

Nonetheless, he could not help but glimpse the sequence of events that had followed the crash. They played out before him like a chimeric motion picture. He watched the arrival of a rescue team in orange parkas, and listened to their radio chatter. He viewed the arrival of the helicopter flickering in dreamlike detail.

He seemed to gain control of the mental projection replay. He relived the crash, again and again, wanting to know every detail. Viewing the newly unveiled memory, he regretted his prior impulsive decision to look away; he had jumped ship prematurely.

Now, immersed in a three dimensional moving memory that played in the theater of his consciousness, he could not look away. He viewed residual energy images over and over until finally they grew faint and then disappeared altogether.

It was then that he discovered something odd—the disturbing images of the past had been superimposed over the present-time crash site. As memories dissipated, the present-time landscape slowly came into view. He perceived yellow police tape fluttering in the wind. A jeep was parked nearby. The mangled tree was... his mind jumped... was that Chase? And Hal?

* * *

The bobcat toyed with the monk, teasing it, slapping it. The tiny icon swung in wider and wider arcs until the string broke and the figure tumbled through the air and plunked sharply off the skull of the meditating hermit.

James looked skyward and caught a glimpse of the bobcat perched above him in the branches, grinning like a Cheshire cat. James, startled, beat a retreat, kicking up a wake of snowflakes. The bobcat leapt down, scampered through the snow in the opposite direction, and sprinted out of sight.

Hal and Chase tried to stifle their laughter, but pent-up emotions exploded into laughter as James sought refuge behind the jeep. Hal plucked the toy monk out of the snow and lofted it to James. "Is this what attacked you?"

The hermit pediatrician lurched forward and fielded the monk figure. Hal followed with a snowball that narrowly missed his off balance shaman. James barely noticed the projectile; he was rolling the tiny monk icon between his fingers, deep in contemplative thought.

Chase joined in and pelted Hal. The two of them battled, launching a volley of frozen missiles. Upon impact, the dry snow exploded into showers of sparking crystals. Soon James joined in and all three carried on gleefully, like schoolchildren on a snow day.

* * *

The trio's uninhibited play set Ray's consciousness vibrating with a "contact high." He watched ghostly forms take shape against the radiant snow, and then recognized the carefree children tumbling in the snow were his friends. Off to one side, an apparition—the baby carriage—flickered in and out of focus.

Pangs of sorrow pummeled Ray. He wanted to join in, wanted to laugh and joke with his friends, but he had been reduced to a phantom they could not see, hear, or touch. He sensed their joy, but could not share it. Was this his fate: to be in the world but never again a part of it? A tsunami of grief washed over Ray, triggering pain. He did not have a body but he was hurting.

Perhaps this was the suffering brought on by attachment that Alice had preached. He was hopelessly attached to his friends, he was attached to the world of sensations and feelings, and now he suffered because his continuing life as a soul had been severed from that world.

But, he argued in his mind, *was it such a bad thing to love worldly things?* Alice once compared life to a game. Ray had balked, but now he wanted to run back out on the playing field. At that moment, he knew he would give anything to reenter the world of the living. He experienced desire at a depth he had not previously imagined possible.

∗ ∗ ∗

James reeled with shock at the vision that blessed his inner eye—Ray sat with his back against the damaged tree staring into space with a lonely smile. James had never before witnessed such sadness. For once in his life, James did not trust his perceptions. I must be slipping, he thought. However, Chase had been watching James and witnessed his face pale to a shade nearly as white as the snow. "James, what's up? You okay?"

* * *

Ray was equally shocked. Was James looking at him? "Can you see me?" But his words did not impinge on the real world.

James squinted, hoping to get a better look. But the vision had faded.

Ray wanted to jump into the arms of James, but instead he shivered as if he had been doused with a bucket of icy water. A host of phantom sprites had descended upon him, the same ones he had passed on his way to the crash site. They grasped Ray gently by the elbows and lifted him to his feet. Alice had warned him: he could refuse the next step in his journey for only so long. His hiatus had expired.

* * *

Chase's cell phone rang. She reached into her pocket but came up empty-handed. Assuming the phone had fallen out during the snowball fight, she searched frantically as urgent rings hammered her with dread.

James and Hal shared a look: *something unusual had happened.*

Chase finally located her phone, dug it out of the snow, and answered the call.

Randi delivered the bad news:

"They're taking him off life support."

* * *

Ray felt his mother's presence, as if she encompassed the space around him like one of Alice's illustrated spheres. He longed to see his mother before his final departure. His thought caused the phantoms to release him. His consciousness hurtled through space. In less than a millisecond he was in a hospital birthing center viewing a mother-to-be. Sweat dampened her brow; labor pains quickened her breathing.

Ray was confused. Was he viewing his mother's memory? Was this the moment of his birth? He concentrated harder. No. The woman wasn't his mother. And the up-to-date computer screens told him he had not traveled back in time.

There was another possibility, but it offered little comfort. *Perhaps he was being reborn.* Maybe the brief embrace with his mother's grief had been her final farewell. Perhaps he had unknowingly stepped back on the merry-go-round of birth and death.

He recalled the baby carriage. Had the image been an invitation for him to begin his earthly life once again? Each thought seemed connected to another in a giant web of meaning. The thoughts and images and emotions all seemed connected: his mother; his new mother; and all mothers.

Between bouts of Lamaze panting the mother-in-labor argued with her husband. Flustered and overcome with emotion, he lobbied to name the boy "Jeff." She preferred "Darian." Ray scanned a series of flashing mental images—the competing names, Jeff and Darian, were embroidered on toddler wear and then on baseball jerseys.

Ray wasn't prepared to be Jeff *or* Darian. He wanted to be Ray. And he would give anything to see his mother, Randi. He blocked out the scene in front of him and replaced it with an image of his mother, much as he had created the image of a balloon in the cabin. He recreated her face, the deep azure of her eyes, the curl of her hair and the smell of her perfume, and memories of his childhood home.

* * *

As he recreated his mother in the blank space of his awareness, he was space-shifted once again. A new scene arose. He remained in the hospital, but in a different room. A woman, head down, clearly distraught, leaned against the wall near the sliding glass doors, phone pressed to her ear. It was Randi.

In the middle of the room, two nurses and a doctor leaned over a lifeless body. Randi averted her gaze, not wanting to view the unfolding medical drama.

Ray shifted his attention to the body. He barely recognized himself. The body, drained of life, was pale and had taken on a yellowish, greenish tint. Unlike Randi, Ray couldn't turn away. As he watched the nurses poke his arms with needles, pry open eyelids, and search for vital signs, an odd thought arose. This vessel or vehicle, home to his beingness for decades, was no longer dear to him. He no longer experienced pangs of remorse. The flesh body that everyone identified as Ray Carte was merely matter that held no life of its own.

In an instant, he experienced a cessation of attachment. He wondered why it had ever been otherwise. All emotion and memory, not to mention all reason and willpower, remained with *him.*

He watched the doctor ease the breathing tube from his throat. A nurse gingerly disconnected an IV line. Another nurse removed a feeding tube. He was ready. It was time.

He wished he could comfort his mother, tell her he was fine and that everything was going to be alright; he wanted desperately to shower Chase with goodbye kisses; he wanted to embrace his friends with one final hug. But he couldn't reach them in any meaningful way; there was nothing left for him to do but let go.

He directed his conscious attention away from the hospital room and once again glimpsed the radiant spirits that both summoned and frightened him, but before he could join their number, a persistent beeping yanked his attention back into the ICU room—

The heart monitor beeped a steady rhythm. But, as seconds passed, the interval between beeps became longer until the monitor hummed a flat line warning.

* * *

On the mountain, Hal, Chase, and James recognized the

sound issuing from the cell phone. Chase bowed her head in defeat. James thought he heard the tree sigh. Had Ray given up?

* * *

Back at the hospital, Father McCarty secured a sobbing Randi in a comforting embrace. Seidman, who passed by on his rounds, nodded silently, signaling he was willing to let the priest handle the mother's grief.

* * *

Alice appeared to Ray. She was no longer teaching. "Ray, you have a decision to make and no time to waste."

An image of his grieving mother flashed, followed by an image of his friends on the mountain, laughing and enjoying life. He didn't have to think for long. He wanted back in the game. He didn't have to tell Alice.

He hit a black wall with a cosmic gut-wrenching impact that shattered his mind. Like a boxer staggered by a knockout blow, pain flooded his splintered consciousness.

Just when he thought he could bear it no longer, the agony receded. But he was rendered paralyzed. He couldn't move, breathe, or see. Had they buried him alive? Was he in a coffin?

* * *

The heart monitor beeped. A tiny spike broke the flat line,

then another and another. A platoon of nurses arrived. Dr. Sloane shouted urgent directions at his team.

* * *

On the mountain, the beeps rang out in the clear air.
"Is that what I think it is?" Hal asked.
James nodded.
They waited for confirmation.

* * *

Randi handed her phone to Fr. McCarty while she scanned Ray's body for signs of life. Had his lip quivered or was that wishful thinking?

* * *

Chase heard Father McCarty's voice, soft but clear with intention: "Get your blessed butts down that mountain. We need you *here*."
Chase and Hal ran for the jeep. James clambered up the incline and returned, clutching the monk.

* * *

Ray struggled, in the dark, suffocated by a crushing weight.

He could not feel a thing. Had he been locked in a steamer trunk that had been dumped to the bottom of the ocean? Had he landed, disembodied, in yet another purgatory? Had he been reborn? Was he still in his new mother's womb? A faint beeping noise reached his ears, then a voice.

"Ray. Ray can you hear us? Can you move your index finger? If you can hear us, wiggle your finger."

Emotions flooded Ray's mind. Fear. Anxiety. Relief. Joy. *He was back.* He had returned and once again was Ray Carte—but he couldn't move the anchor that was his body. He had to let them know, but he could not feel his fingers or find his voice.

* * *

Lani recognized Ray was regaining a tenuous grasp on consciousness—would he succeed in making his way back? Only time could tell. Randi, too, sensed that Ray was trying to say something. Dr. Sloane watched patiently until Ray finally moved his index finger.

Pain returned like a lightning strike, first in his head, but soon the fire radiated and stabbed at every limb. Still, he had to try to let them know he was alive. It took Herculean concentration to raise an eyebrow.

"Beautiful," said Lani. "That's wonderful. We can see you."

"Take it easy, Ray." Dr. Sloane's voice was steady and reassuring. "We're in no hurry."

It took nearly five minutes, but Ray managed to open

his right eye, then his left. His vision was clouded; he could barely make out the outlines of four figures standing over him. Like a scuba diver rising from the depths, he saw only a sea of washed out colors—blue, white and yellow beams swimming above him. Slowly, the world came into focus and took shape. Before long, he was peering into his mother's eyes. *I love you.* She didn't respond. *I love you.* Ray strained to form the intention, but no one answered.

He wasn't with Alice anymore. He was back in the physical world. They couldn't hear his thoughts. He had to use his voice, not his mind. He marshaled his remaining strength to speak, but that which had been so effortless just a short time ago, when he was outside the body, now taxed his ability.

"Alice—" he whispered. It wasn't what he meant to say. Why was there a disconnect between his thoughts and his speech?

Dr. Sloane cut him off, "Don't worry, Ray, you're in good hands." Turning to Randi, he explained the situation: "We won't know if he suffered brain damage, or to what extent. He needs time to recover. We'll perform some simple tests."

Randi could no longer fight the tears streaming down her face.

"Alice told me," Ray stammered.

"Ray, it's important you rest." Father McCarty stepped forward. His kindly face and gentle smile calmed Ray's nerves.

Randi spoke through broken sobs. "Get a little rest, honey, then you can tell us everything."

Ray's head sunk deeper into the pillow as he relaxed. He winked. He wanted to tell his mother that he loved her, he wanted to see Chase, and he desperately wanted to tell them all that he had learned from Alice, but pain blocked his efforts. So this was the price of his decision to return—pain, and lots of it.

That's alright, he thought as he closed his eyes. He was willing to pay the price. With his mother holding his hand, he fell into a deep restful sleep.

23

For two days, Hal and Chase maintained a vigil by Ray's bedside. Barely ten words were spoken between them as Ray drifted in and out of consciousness. James stopped by a few times to say hello and Eva showed up nearly every day with Bren.

By the afternoon of the third day, Ray awoke and remained alert. The group basked in the warmth of his impending recovery, though the ordeal was far from over. They knew Ray had a long way to go—and it was still somewhat painful for him to talk.

One afternoon, after an emotionally exhausting reunion, they let Ray rest. Chase stayed by his bed. Randi sat in the far corner, reading *Alice's Adventures in Wonderland* to Bren. Ray appreciated the warmth of his mother's voice and pretended he was back in his childhood room. Ten-year-old Bren was transported into a magical world by the story.

Chase admired the bond developing between Bren and Randi, but her thoughts kept wandering to her secret, to her pregnancy. Would she be half as good a mother as Randi had been to Ray? Would she have handled the crisis with as much grace?

She was jolted out of her reverie when Ray squeezed her hand. A memory had awakened him. He made an effort to speak, wanting to tell Chase about his experience, or was it merely his dream? He needed to tell her about Alice and the cabin and the beast and his father and… her wedding dress. He needed confirmation that he had not been hallucinating. His recall was already somewhat fragmented, like broken light streaming through a stained-glass window. He redoubled his effort to remain alert, battling the torpor induced by painkillers.

Chase leaned close, aware he was struggling.

He managed a whisper, "Baby, baby carriage…"

Chase flushed and stammered, "How… how did you know?"

"How did I know?" Ray was confused.

"How did you know I was pregnant?"

Ray puzzled: *she was pregnant?* That explained the baby carriage. But how could he explain perceiving a reality in his post-mortem state that he could not have known in the physical world?

"How long…"

Chase kissed his cheek. "Not now. When you're rested." She sealed her promise by squeezing his hand. She had feigned nonchalance but, nonetheless, was perplexed. Ray had unintentionally drawn her into his strange world.

Ray drifted asleep, transported by painkillers. Hours later a brusque orderly piloted a gurney into the room. With the social graces of a robot, he announced that he had orders to transport "a Mr. Ray Carte" to Imaging for a brain scan.

Randi, who had been stroking Bren's hair as the girl slept, attempted to derail his mission. "That has to be done now?"

"Dr. Sloane ordered the tests. They'll only take an hour. Or maybe a little longer."

Two nurse assistants helped the orderly transfer Ray, who was still half asleep, to the gurney. Without further ado, he was whisked out of the room and down the hall. In less than twenty minutes, he was encapsulated in an MRI machine being assaulted by the ear-smacking thumps of the giant magnets. Reclining in the narrow tunnel of the giant imaging machine induced claustrophobia. Ray tried to visualize the hi-tech magic involved, the capture of image slices a molecule wide, but the exercise failed to calm his nerves.

Instead, he meditated on the mystery of his encounter with Alice: the mountain cabin; the lessons; the tea; and Biscuit. The details felt real but wasn't that the case with vivid dreams? Before the accident he had dismissed the idea of a near-death experience but *wasn't that exactly what had happened?*

He had spent his academic career ridiculing such scientifically unsound ideas. And yet, now that he had been at death's door, his prior assumptions had been shaken. Something profound had no doubt taken place. His usual arsenal of arguments had been neutered. For the first time, he understood the certainty of those who visited the other side. *Something had happened.*

He was fully awake and alert by the time the radiologist cheerfully declared, "It's a wrap. I see nothing remarkable.

I'll send the images to your doctor. He'll discuss the results with you."

"Great."

The gruff orderly returned, helped Ray slide onto the gurney, and sped out of Imaging but he miscalculated the turn… and the gurney glanced off the doorjamb with a jarring thud that elicited a moan from Ray. The orderly regained control, but Ray signaled for him to halt.

Though Ray's voice was faint, he found he could make himself heard. "Hey, speedy. Can we take a detour? There's something I need to check out."

"No can do. Have to stick with the routes."

Ray continued, engaging in creative storytelling, taking ample pauses to catch his breath. "I'm dying. I'm on the way out. I have one last wish—a short visit to glimpse the new arrivals. Seeing those happy little fellas… will give me a huge lift. You've got no idea… how depressed—"

"Sorry to hear you're not doing so well, but—"

"Okay, you're a professional. I get it. Listen, you're a decent gurney driver… but that bump back there—"

"Thomas. Name is Thomas."

"Thomas. I think we could agree… you deserve a tip… even with the little mishap. When we get back, I've got a portrait of Jackson… that's yours."

Ray listened as the squeaking gurney wheels rolled on for another twenty paces. As they approached the end of the hallway, the stretcher slowed.

"Promise you'll stay behind the glass? Swear you won't tell anyone?"

Ray nodded his assent.

Thomas executed a three-point turn, shoved the gurney into an elevator. One floor up, he exited the elevator and rolled the gurney down a lengthy corridor to a waiting room adjacent to the nursery. Large viewing windows opened onto a nursery where newborns slept.

"You good, pal?" Thomas asked as he parked the gurney against the glass partition.

Ray winced with pain as he propped himself on one elbow and peered at rows of cradled napping infants. In the far corner, two jaundiced infants were bathed with fluorescent glow from a light therapy box.

"Good. I'm good." Ray groaned.

Thomas extracted a pack of cigarettes from his pocket and ducked into a nearby restroom.

Ray thought the nursery looked familiar; it was a room he had remote viewed during his NDE. It was adjacent to the room where the mother had been in labor. Then again, perhaps all maternity wards looked the same. He needed time to reflect and assess—had his out-of-body experience been real? How would he ever tell?

A weary father in a cardigan sweater maintained a droopy-eyed vigil, shuffling past Ray's gurney. On his third pass he studied Ray and quipped, "What the heck happened to you, pal?"

Ray forced a smile. He scrutinized the man's features and found them familiar, and that sweater—he *knew* that sweater. He was positive—this man had argued with his wife about naming their son.

Though exhausted, the new father was giddy and enjoyed kidding Ray. "What happened? You try to coach your wife through labor?"

They both chuckled, though Ray ended up grimacing with rib pain.

"Which one is Jeff?" Ray whispered.

The father in the cardigan proudly pointed out a healthy pink infant tucked securely in his ward crib.

"Jeff. That's a good name. Better than Darian," Ray said.

The man stuttered. "Wha…what did you say? Darian? My wife never discussed the name Darian with anyone. She brought it up during labor—that was the only time. How did you know? Who *are* you?"

The new father turned a hard stare on the strange injured man on the gurney.

Ray's heart raced. First it was Chase and the baby carriage, and now this man. Details. His recall was being confirmed. He was not sure if that was a good thing. Was the foundation on which he had previously built his world now crumbling? Was a world that was normally hidden from view now being revealed?

Before the new father could sort through his confusion, Thomas returned, reeking of tobacco smoke. Ray waved good-bye to Jeff's father, who was brewing suspicions. Ray tried to appear normal in order to dispel the father's fear— the man must wonder if Ray was a baby-snatching psycho-path. Thomas tugged the gurney and they sailed down the hall before the awkward encounter escalated.

On the way back to his room, Ray tried to think of logical

explanations for the events that had just happened. He was back in the physical world. Alice clearly had not been a figment of his imagination, but what was she? He needed to talk to someone, someone real.

24

Randi escorted Les Crane into the room. Ray was sitting up, drinking orange juice through a straw. Ray shook Les' extended hand and fixed on the pink unicorn lapel pin.

"If you prefer, I can return later," said Les, misinterpreting the pause. "Although we have found it is best to document the near-death experience as soon as possible."

"Stay," Ray said. Though he was not certain he should share his story with a stranger, Les seemed like a pleasant fellow. "Mother said you were someone I could speak to honestly. Said you had experience and you weren't likely to—"

"Insist you're crazy?"

"Something like that," Ray chuckled. Randi fluffed a pillow and propped it up behind him.

Ray composed himself. "I would like to share my experience. Yet, I know how hard it is for others to accept what I have to say. Not too long ago, I thought this kind of thing sounded crazy, so I don't expect anyone to believe me. But it doesn't matter who believes… what happened is what it is. Nothing more, nothing less."

Les shed his coat. With rehearsed precision he fetched a

recorder from his leather satchel, opened a fresh spiral note-book, and uncapped his Mount Blanc fountain pen. His polished manner put Ray at ease.

Still, Ray had doubts. He could picture the tabloid headline: "Crackpot Claims Life After Death." How could anyone grasp what he had been through—unless they had lived through the same experience? He thought of the Ray Carte he had once been, that Ray would have run a thorough background check on Les before they even met. But then, if Ray had been his old self, there would be no way he would talk to a paranormal researcher in the first place.

Randi sensed Ray's lingering discomfort.

"Dear, Les was recommended by a friend."

"Is this off the record?"

"If you want your interview to be anonymous, we can do that. Because so many people benefit from my work, I'm happy to conduct an interview on a confidential basis, when necessary. I'll use your interview in my research, but you'll remain anonymous."

"See, your story may help someone else," Randi jumped in.

"Also, while I'm not a licensed therapist, many people find sharing their experience has therapeutic value. Once they unburden they often discover they're not alone. If someone doesn't know that others have had the same experience, they may fear they've lost their minds."

"Not sure I can make sense of what happened," Ray offered.

"I'm not here to judge the validity of your claims. I'm here to listen and document your account of what took place after you slipped into a coma."

Ray sipped his orange juice and contemplated the next step. Les was tightly wound, but he seemed genuine. Besides, Ray realized, he might never have another opportunity to speak candidly with someone who might understand.

"After the crash, I left my body, suddenly. You know what I mean?"

Les nodded.

"I experienced being outside, separate. I didn't want to feel the pain. This desire to escape was something I could not have anticipated."

Les nodded *go on*.

"Almost immediately, I found myself in a different setting. Yet I was not alone. Someone was there with me."

"Who?"

"I called her Alice."

"Alice?"

"Like Alice in Wonderland."

"Interesting."

"I know she wasn't really Alice," Ray continued. "Perhaps beings or angels on the other side take forms we easily rec-ognize. Maybe they appear in a way that does not frighten us. Maybe I saw Alice because my mother used to read that story to me."

Randi showed Les the book she had been reading to Bren.

"Yes, of course. Thank you." Les seemed to take the fact with some hesitancy.

Ray continued: "Anyway, so someone was there, like a teacher, but much more, like a spirit guide. She was an angel, but not like we usually think of angels. She taught lessons.

Only we did not talk, we shared thought pictures."

Les leaned forward and scribbled a note. "Were you in a classroom of sorts? Or in a fantastical environment?"

"Let me start at the beginning." Ray delivered a step-by-step account, starting with his encounter with the girl who sat under the tree. It took nearly two hours. He then provided Les with details regarding the hospital medical team's resuscitation efforts—which he could have known only if he had been in the room. Finished with his account, he relaxed his head against the pillow.

"Tell me more about your decision to return," Les said.

"It was Alice… she convinced me," Ray replied. He was about to elaborate when Dr. Seidman entered, anxious to share his dark mood. He fixed Les with a hostile stare.

"Sir, can I speak with you? Outside."

Randi was busy counting to ten with her eyes closed, trying to make the unpleasantness disappear by sheer will-power.

Les conceded the battle and turned to follow the psychologist into the hall, but Seidman pointed at Les' paraphernalia. "Bring your gear, please."

Ray looked at his mother for an explanation. Randi shook her head: *let it go.*

On his way out, Les tapped the railing of Ray's bed. "Ray, we'll see each other again. I always conduct follow-ups."

Once they were in the hall and safely out of earshot, Seidman berated Les. "What do you think you're doing? The patient suffered major trauma. He's vulnerable and open to suggestion, and you feed him carnival hocus-pocus. Do you have any idea of the damage you could cause? After the hospital releases my patient, I can't stop you. But while he's in this hospital, I'm responsible. We're done here. Please leave."

"Thank you, I appreciate your hospitality. I'll be sure to mention it in forthcoming publications." He turned and made his way to the elevator.

Seidman's complexion reddened. He took a deep breath before reentering Ray's room.

Once he arrived at Ray's bedside he tried to change gears, "Sorry about that distraction. I did not have a chance to introduce myself. I'm Dr. Seidman, the psychologist assigned—"

"Pull up a chair. Can I offer you a cup of coffee? Might have to bribe a nurse," Ray joked.

"Thanks, but I've had my fill of caffeine for the day."

The nurse assistant clearing Ray's food tray hid her smile. She could tell Ray was prepared to toss jabs in Seidman's direction. Though the staff had witnessed the dust-up with Les, no one dared mention it. They were practiced in the art of avoiding the psychologist.

Seidman turned to Randi. "Might you leave us alone for a few minutes?"

Randi sighed and took her leave. Another confrontation was the last thing she needed. Knowing Ray's penchant for heated argument, she thought about warning him to take it easy, but Seidman stood like a sentry over the bed.

"What can I do for you doctor?" Ray asked. "I don't recall requesting the services of a psychologist." The words were sharper than Ray had intended; his displeasure with the man's manner had seeped into his voice. After all, the shrink had dismissed both his guest and his mother with discourteous aplomb.

"I want you to know that I'm here for you, if you want to discuss your experience. It can be hard for patients to process the difficult emotions of a traumatic event, like your accident." Ray's aloof response motivated him to continue. "At times I may appear abrupt, but I assure you it's only because I care. Some people have been known to take advantage of medical trauma to… Well, you know what I mean."

Ray understood the implication, but chose to remain silent.

"We've made advances," the psychologist continued. "We have a better understanding of the unusual perceptions experienced during trauma. We now recognize the psychological side effects. In the past, we simply dismissed the emotional scars. If we said anything at all, we assured patients they would forget, if not right away, then eventually. However, we were mistaken. They didn't always forget. Many became upset, troubled."

"I can imagine."

"So now I try to make sure that my patients benefit from our improved knowledge. They need to know what happened to them, so they can move on with their lives."

Ray smoothed the bed sheets, a gesture that signaled his lack of interest. Though Ray bristled at Seidman's rudeness, he had also recognized a part of himself in the doctor. He, too, had been a "rational man" armed with prepackaged explanations for any encounters with the unusual or with the paranormal. Just one week ago, he might have sided with the psychologist, but not today. Instead, he resented the assumption that he lacked sufficient sophistication to discern between fantasy and reality. Nonetheless, he tempered his response.

"Excellent," Ray said, patronizing the therapist. "Good approach. I'm glad you're on top of it. Never hurts to stay up on the latest."

"We've realized the brain is capable of much more than we ever imagined. In fact, so much more that—we're not certain we'll ever understand entirely. But that doesn't leave us empty-handed. We start with what we know and then we go forward based on inferences."

Alice had delivered an amazingly accurate critique of this line of thinking, Ray noted.

Seidman continued the lecture, "For example, the brain is capable of cobbling together memories to create imaginary scenarios."

"Imaginary scenarios?" asked Ray.

"The brain seeks coherent reason. Sometimes it must construct elaborate scenarios to make everything hang together. It creates fantasies that help us survive, emotionally. The brain is focused on survival. If we think we're dying, what does the brain do?"

"No idea. Tell me. What does the brain do?"

"It manufactures imaginary scenarios that assure us that we'll never die. It protects us emotionally. Of course, we do not survive death, but the brain helps us *believe* we will survive. It creates scenarios to help us cope. Sometimes they're religious scenarios that promise immortality. When people are no longer assured they'll live, when they fear death, the brain invents survival. Remarkable, isn't it?"

"Fascinating. I didn't know that."

Seidman had anticipated greater resistance. Many patients were unwilling to let go of their delusions; he figured Ray was one. Such people, in spite of all his arguments, insisted they had a real experience and rejected the idea they experienced a fantasy cobbled together by bruised gray matter. The psychologist considered their denial proof of the chameleon-like nature of the brain, which was a master at disguising its operations.

"I wasn't aware brain research had progressed that far," Ray conceded. "I find it quite amazing that they have identified the actual neurons and synapses that fabricate out-of-body experiences. It's amazing they can read the actual program in the brain."

Was Ray putting him on? Seidman wasn't certain. In spite of his doubts, he continued, "There are places in the brain… stimulating those locations causes an illusion of an out-of-body experience. For short periods of time."

"How long?"

"Two seconds."

"Not very long. How do they know their poking causes a mere illusion? Maybe their poking and stimulating creates actual trauma. And that trauma causes the soul to separate from the body."

"Simple cause-and-effect. Stimulate the brain, get an out-of-body report. Cause and effect."

"Hold on. That doesn't prove the experience is an illusion. The probing might cause an actual separation."

"Yes, I see your point. But where is the soul or spirit? Nowhere. No one ever sees the spirit. It doesn't exist."

"Ever read Plato?"

"I don't recall," Seidman said.

Ray didn't believe him for a second. "You don't recall the story about the cave?"

"I may have heard about it."

"Plato speculated that we're like the inhabitants of a cave. What we perceive as reality is only shadows cast upon the wall by light streaming into the cave. We become mesmerized and look in only one direction where we see only the shadows cast by the light. We do not see the light. But a few brave souls exit the cave and see the light. They see reality as it is."

Dr. Seidman withheld comment.

Ray continued, "Plato warns us that when the explorers return to the cave with news of their discovery, the others will refuse to believe them. Those brave souls are usually attacked."

"In Plato's day, brain science was pretty crude. That was an age of superstition. Thank goodness we've moved on from those primitive caves."

"So my imagination went on tilt and I experienced a hallucination? And my brain created a fantasy and convinced itself that it was able to survive death? But, ultimately, it was just playing a joke on itself?"

"A patient who recognizes that their experience was imaginary can let it go. They can get on with their life. They gain valuable perspective. But I'm afraid that Les has confused you. Folks like him lure people into a fool's maze. I don't want that to happen to you."

"I appreciate your concern," Ray said. "I wouldn't want to leave the hospital carrying on like a nutcase."

Ray wished Chase had been there, at his side. He wished she had not taken Eva and Bren for dessert at a nearby diner. She had a wicked sense of humor and would have backed him up. When it came to hostile social encounters, they formed a brutal tag team.

The psychologist had become increasingly tense. It dawned on him that his intervention was not going as well as he had hoped.

Ray, on the other hand, had made his point: though the doctor might believe that Ray was deluded, at least the doctor knew he was dealing with an opponent who could debate the diagnosis. Nonetheless, a total absence of understanding and trust separated the two men.

The psychologist now understood that his patient was determined to hold his cards close to his chest and was not about to confide in the doctor. As Seidman exited, he offered a parting truce, "Listen, if you need someone to talk with, I'm here for you. If you don't, that's okay."

Ray toasted the doctor with his cup of orange juice, and then laid his head back on his pillow. It had been a stressful hour. He needed rest.

* * *

Hours later, Ray opened his eyes. How long had he been

asleep? He searched for a clock but didn't find one. The room was empty. Where was Chase? He wished he could float and transport himself wherever he intended.

As minutes passed in silence, he grew restless. The pain in his joints was annoying, in spite of the cocktail of painkillers that clouded his brain. The weight of his body had become oppressive, a stark contrast to floating through space. During the time he spent with Alice, he had suffered vertigo and disorientation. Now he didn't know which was worse: losing contact with the physical world or being tied down by it. Previously, Ray had not thought of gravity as an enemy, but now he cursed the force.

Though he tried to remember his lessons with Alice, he only heard Seidman's voice in his head. What if the psychologist was right? What if his recall was an elaborate hallucination, the product of altered brain chemicals? Another voice joined the internal argument: how could he have known the baby's name? How could he have known things that were verifiable? The first voice retorted: maybe he had jumped to conclusions, maybe he had misinterpreted…

Ray rubbed his closed eyes. He had to stop the hot debate raging in his head like an annoying talk show segment. It was stretching his nerves to their limit. He tried to remember the lessons; the lessons were all that mattered.

Whether Alice had been a spiritual guide or a product of his subconscious, she had taught him to control his mind. She had coached him to discern between his thoughts and thoughts projected by others. He knew that if he hoped to still the noise in his head, he must track his mental creations from moment to moment and seek to be fully present.

The balloon exercise came to mind. The task now proved harder. After a few minutes, he managed only a weak projection. Nevertheless, he felt lighter, less burdened by gnawing doubts. He had almost drifted to sleep when an angry voice startled him.

"I received a complaint."

Ray opened his eyes as Seidman entered once again.

"It wasn't really a complaint. It was an inquiry."

"Go on…" Ray said.

"A very upset father in the maternity ward called security wanting to know how a trauma patient that he had never seen before could know the name of his newborn child. He wanted to know how that patient knew a name that he and his wife rejected, a name they discussed only in private. He wanted to know if the hospital was bugged. He asked why we did not have adequate security and why we were lax when it came to his family's safety."

"Curious."

Seidman bristled, "I could have referred the matter to the proper authorities, but I decided to show a little courtesy and ask you directly how you knew those names. We know you bribed an orderly. Did you bribe a maternity nurse?"

Ray had reached his limit with the confrontation. The drugs in his system shortened his fuse. He recognized that he was in dangerous territory; he knew his anger might erupt. He was not in the mood to be interrogated. Yet, his encounter with Alice had humbled him and had taught him to control his temper.

"Maybe it had to do with neurons wanting to survive," he said, acting puzzled.

The frustrated psychologist spun on his heel and exited once again.

Ray exhaled. Though he took pride in his restraint, he feared what might happen next. The real danger was not the man's willingness to sit in an unlit cave; the danger was his passion for insisting others join him in that dark place.

Lani, who had overheard the entire exchange, entered, smoothed Ray's pillow, and winked encouragement. "Doctor Sloane said you're progressing well. You should be out of here tomorrow, or the next day at the latest."

"Thank you," Ray sighed, grateful for some good news.

It had been a trying recovery and he knew it would take time before he was back to normal. At least he was going home where he could focus on the things that mattered: the baby, the start-up venture, maybe even writing a book. He had decided it was time to stop stalling; he and Chase had delayed their future for long enough.

And, besides, who knew when he would be called back to the cabin with Alice, torn away from everyone dear to him. Who knew when he would be forced to put in another appearance on the other side, beyond this life? It was time to kick life into high gear.

25

Ray and Chase arrived at the cabin nestled in a breathtaking mountain meadow that resembled a Bierstadt painting. James greeted them with unexpected solemnity and gestured toward the woods. Angry volleys of expletives shattered the alpine serenity. After each round of curses, rocks ricocheted off tree trunks. Hal was on a tear.

"What the heck is going on?" Ray set out to investigate. He found his best friend perched on a boulder, swearing and hurling stones.

"That double-crossing lowlife."

"You talking about me?" Ray joked, hoping to defuse the tension.

Hal wrapped him in a bear hug.

"You won't believe what that snake of a psychologist did," Hal said. "I don't want you to think for one second that you're responsible, not in any way. You hear? You're not taking this personally."

"What happened?"

"They pulled our funding. That freak cast major doubt on you—on your ability to run the program. He soiled our reservoir of goodwill. He told the board you might suffer 'long-term' disability as a result of your accident. He convinced them that 'you can no longer be counted on.'"

Ray recalled that when his mother had told him that Seidman held a position on the board that oversaw his funding, he had experienced trepidation. Those fears had been prophetic.

"When I get done with him…" Hal threatened.

"I hardly told him anything," Ray said. "He copped an attitude. Guess I should have known he would scuttle our program."

Hal tossed another rock.

"I'm sorry," Ray said. "This messes you up, doesn't it? You've been waiting and now it comes to this—to nothing."

"Not your fault."

Ray sought to offer comfort, but couldn't find the words. Though he was disheartened, he knew Hal needed the start-up more than he did. Hal was fully invested. He had gambled on the venture and now was in a tight spot.

"Is everything okay?" Chase called from the cabin.

"Yeah, fine. A fine mess."

Ray turned to Hal. "Let's not spoil the afternoon for James. Don't say a thing. Let's have a nice tea ceremony. We'll think of something. Maybe we'll sue. Let's head on back."

Ray needed time to think. *Did he have a legal case against the psychologist? Maybe.* One thing was sure: he resented the intense hatred aimed at him. He wondered about motive, and hatched a hunch: he had threatened the psychologist's fundamental view of reality based on materialism. Ray's NDE account had been a jackhammer tearing up the foundation under Seidman's feet.

The accident was now many months in the rearview mirror. Ray's life had changed in many ways: he was engaged; he was an expectant father; he was a budding author; and he had acquired a calm, introspective demeanor. One thing had not changed: his passion for ferreting out a sleazy opponent's moves. Ray vowed to set things right.

As Hal and Ray exited the woods and neared the cabin where Chase and James were waiting, Les pulled up in his beat-up, sun-faded Volvo.

Ray mused out loud, sharing his thoughts with Hal. "When Seidman heard I was helping Les with his research, he launched his vendetta. Les is the one man who truly annoys him."

"Maybe you should take a pass on sharing your story," Hal suggested.

Ray dismissed the idea with a shake of his head. He was in no mood to retreat.

Moments later, when they arrived at the cabin, James was escorting Les on a royal tour of his one-room abode. Randi tended boiling water and fussed over preparing loose leaf tea. Chase saw Ray and frowned an unspoken question: *what's up?*

Ray escorted Chase outside to a grassy rise overlooking the creek, a glistening crystal ribbon splitting the meadow. The snow was melting, but spring was weeks away; it was one of those late winter days when the sun shines hot but the frozen earth continues its wintry repose.

"What's up with Hal?" she pressed.

"A minor setback. Nothing serious."

"Oh. I thought he might have a good reason for cursing and attacking those poor trees."

"The accident changed all of us," Ray said, wrapping her in a supportive hug. "I was thinking… We ought to make some changes. You know how easy it is to get stuck. One day follows the next and before you know it, you're in a rut."

Chase frowned her concern.

"Getting stuck in a rut is one of my shortcomings," he continued. "The accident knocked me out of my rut. And now I don't want to fall back."

Chase puzzled. *Where was he going with this monologue? Was this about the wedding? Had he undergone a change of heart?*

"Are we set for next week?" he asked.

She nodded, her worry doubling.

"What about Father McCarty? He'll deliver the vows?" Ray asked.

"He promised to make arrangements."

"And Bren found a dress? I had no idea she would be so ecstatic to be a flower girl."

"You have a funny way of getting out of ruts. What's up? C'mon, fess up."

He snorted and shook his head dismissively. "They cancelled our funding. We're out of business. Hal was a tad bit upset."

Chase blinked as if she had been punched in the nose.

"Doesn't change our plans," said Ray. "The marriage has

nothing to do with business or funding. When I was on that mountain, I was certain beyond any possible doubt that I wanted us to have a future together."

"While you were in a coma? Not a good time to make major, life-altering decisions."

"The best time," he countered. "At one point, my thoughts were totally synchronized with Alice's thoughts. A good marriage must be like that—making decisions in unison that create life and a world."

She began to see the picture he was painting.

"When I thought I was about to start life over as a baby, I watched as new parents experienced amazing feelings. They witnessed the beginning of a life in which they played a role. We should feel that kind of joy every single day—"

"We're doing just that," she said, resting her hand on her expanding belly.

"We are. We're creating a life moment to moment." He paused. "I probably sound like a soapbox preacher."

"No, I understand." She drew a breath. "Your mother worried that her bad marriage messed you up for good. She feared it would be difficult for you to make a relationship work. She thought the trauma of her divorce left scars rendering you unfit for domestic life."

"I hope she can let that go. My father was ill, in a strange way. His soul festered with evil. It was like living with a rabid dog. We never knew when he might bite."

There was nothing Chase could add. She knew Ray had to deal with the past on his own terms. Many times, late into the night, he had talked about how to make destructive emotions vanish. He had talked about overcoming desire and attachment. She had no doubt he would figure out how to overcome the latest setback.

"Will Hal be okay?" she asked.

"He'll be fine. We put everything into our pitch, so when it comes to money, we're screwed. But it'll work out." Ray paused. "Seidman torpedoed the deal. He fostered doubt by insinuating that I was unstable. He's the type of person… He's a dream killer."

"He resented you talking with Les? Maybe you're inviting trouble."

"No. We should not surrender. I want to share my experience. Let's get back. They'll be waiting for us. Are you ready for a tea ceremony with James?"

"Not sure I'll ever be ready."

"It'll keep us out of the rut."

* * *

James hosted an elaborate ceremony. Ray allowed his thoughts to wander during the meditative silence. His consciousness flowed freely between the banks formed by the sights and sounds of James' cabin: the swirling tea; the pungent odor of the wood-burning stove; the rumble of the creek; dust motes dancing in the light that streamed through unwashed windows.

He reflected on the quality of the light, that most mysterious phenomenon. *Light was sometimes a wave, sometimes a particle; it always travelled at the same speed in a vacuum, no matter how fast an observer was traveling. It was an electrical field and a magnetic field entangled in a vibrating dance. It was a carrier of communications and aesthetics. Its mysteries dazzled the rational mind.*

Ray then turned his attention inward, allowing intense emotions to bubble to the surface. Wave after wave of emotion washed over him, until finally he rested in the bliss of simply being there without attachment.

When Ray studied James, he imagined the recluse was a magician orchestrating events with an unseen hand. James returned Ray's look: he mirrored the thought, believing Ray was secretly the magician in charge. Ray recalled Alice's lesson—we orchestrate reality in concert with others. James, it seemed to Ray, appreciated the subtle tapestry of creation, its shared spiritual origin. Ray vowed to spend more time with the physician medicine man.

Conversations with James would no doubt differ from the talk he was about to have with Les. While James was a fearless explorer traveling up a river into the dark jungle, Les catalogued specimens. His game was classification, while James sought realms beyond category and class.

Ray, surrounded by close friends, allowed his mind to surf on contentment and peace. And then, at the end of the ceremony, Ray toasted their wedding plans. Formalizing his union with Chase united those gathered. When two people pledged mutual support "for better or worse," their act renewed a primal hope all men and women shared—hope that a loving and lasting partnership was possible. It was this hope that kept humankind stumbling into the future with heads held high.

Hal, his anger purged, blurted out news of the funding collapse, adding a stoic twist to the bad news. He claimed events had turned out for the best. Luck had been on their side. "If the cancellation had happened later, Ray and I would have suffered more, as our hearts and souls would've been totally immersed in the program. Once we had achieved success, these scoundrels would have trashed our dreams. It was better to have them expose their true colors before we enjoyed success."

Hal raised his cup in a toast. "Ray, my good and decent partner, you smoked them out."

Ray lifted his cup, "Here's to glorious poverty."

Everyone joined in, "Hear, hear."

James kneaded a serious thought and then announced, "I've a bit of news to add. Up until now, I've kept this information to myself. This past week I completed the purchase of the land in this valley."

"All of it?" Chase asked, with unguarded shock.

"We weren't sure you even owned this cabin," Hal retorted.

"To be honest, we thought you were a homesteader," Ray confessed.

"Plans have been in the works for a couple years. I'm building a spiritual retreat."

Ray initiated another toast. "To your success."

"No, to *our* success. I would be extremely honored to have your help with this dream project. And, given you're both out of work, I can afford your time," he joked.

The surprise announcement was one of life's mysterious reversals of fortune: the announcement transformed misfortune into bounty. James had turned lead into gold.

Ray met the reversal of fortune with an open heart and mind; he sensed that something unusual, something just beyond his awareness, was taking root and sprouting into existence.

26

Ray and Les hiked upstream to an idyllic setting where the creek widened and carved a sandy beach into the rocky landscape. Smooth boulders seemed to have been perfectly positioned for the comfort of weary hikers. Rays of sunlight glinted off the glassy surface of tranquil pools.

Les settled on a rock with his back to the creek; his body baffled the rumble of the cascading water, protecting the inexpensive microphone he set up for the interview.

Ray selected a smooth, flat-topped boulder, and settled in. He closed his eyes and turned his face to the sun, welcoming the solar balm he hoped would heal the residual scars on his forehead.

Originally, Les had scheduled the interview to take place at James' tea ceremony but time had run out that eventful day. Now, three months later, they were finally about to record the interview.

Les spoke into his microphone, "This is The Pink Unicorn, a podcast that seeks answers to paranormal questions. Today I'll interview Ray Carte, a man who experienced the near-death state after a horrific automobile crash on an icy road.

Ray, will you tell us what happened to you?"

Les listened closely as Ray recounted the accident and his experience. Twenty minutes later, Les prompted, "Ray, I'm sure our listeners would like to hear more about Alice. She sounds fascinating."

"At one point, Alice transformed into a monk," Ray explained. "At the time, I thought that maybe I had once been a monk devoted to spiritual pursuits. Perhaps I had broken away from the monastic tradition to live subsequent lifetimes fully attached to the mundane world. I don't know for sure if that was true. But it did occur to me that my experience was some kind of wake-up call designed to put me back in touch with my true nature."

"Maybe your past helped you comprehend her lessons?"

"Well, I know she considered me a difficult student, someone who required remedial work. She seemed to want me to remember my past, but didn't order me to return to the life of a monk. Anyway, I discovered it was difficult to disperse the black clouds of amnesia. It wasn't easy for me to recall my past."

"Was that the essence of the lessons?" Les asked, savoring every detail.

"I'm not sure. But I know they were strictly remedial. She wanted me to untie the knots that had kept me in bondage to illusions. She wanted me to disentangle my spiritual mind from attachments. She pushed me to pull up anchors I had buried in temporal mud."

"Were you able to make progress?"

"Barely. She simply led me to the trailhead where the real

path begins. I must admit I did not get very far this time."

"But you're doing okay?"

"Pretty much. Some people have become upset when I talk about what happened. A psychologist at the hospital spread rumors that I was unstable because I spoke of the near-death experience. That cost me my new business. But I learned that kind of fear is common."

"The scold was Dr. Seidman?"

"Yes. He was the one," Ray replied. "I'm guessing that some very personal reason caused him to act so badly. His concerns seemed odd: he was worried I would become disillusioned with mundane life; he feared daily responsibilities might tax my patience; he was worried I would have less tolerance for disappointment. None of that has been a problem. Life has been better than good. But few people want to discuss what happened to me."

"That leaves you feeling lonely?"

"No, not at all. But I have learned you have to be careful what you say. People like Seidman will drug you or lock you up if you disturb their prejudices."

"So you decided to keep a low profile?"

"I prefer intimate conversations over coffee. I prefer conversations that take place while walking along mountain streams. Or while watching sunsets. In the past, monks who possessed this ancient knowledge were sequestered in caves or cloistered in monasteries. But that time has passed. And yet, perhaps these matters are meant only for those who enjoy contemplation and prayer. Patience, it turns out, is an acquired virtue."

"Fortunately, Ray, more and more individuals are seeking spiritual insight."

* * *

Later that afternoon, after Ray's narrative came to a close, Les spoke about his research. Though Ray's experience was unique, in the way that any personal experience is unique, it was also similar to other cases Les had investigated. Les explained that others who had experienced near death also reported visiting an ideational world where thoughts, viewed in picture form, could be shared telepathically. Others also encountered guides that had functioned as religious teachers. When religious figures had been encountered, they had rarely declared their identity.

Les explained how other subjects who had experienced near death could change location; they could appear and disappear, at will. It had seemed to them that intentions dictated their movement. Many had viewed from a position outside their body—they reported out-of-body experiences or OBE's. Emotional concerns, most had discovered, would cause them to view events taking place in the world they left behind. Typically, however, friends and loved ones had failed to detect their presence.

Les turned his attention back to Ray. "I'm impressed with your ability to articulate your insights. Few return with the ability to describe the NDE with such clarity, eloquence and intellectual depth.

"Thank you," Ray said, humbled by the praise.

"Many who survived such an ordeal were left with a radically altered outlook that they were unable to explain. Their ambiguity motivates mainstream scientists to disregard the field."

Research, Les explained, involves tedious boredom punctuated by occasional discovery and euphoria. The work relied on extensive fieldwork, as the study of consciousness rarely could be conducted in the lab. Les joked that inducing death was clearly out of bounds at this time.

Ray sensed that Les might go on for hours, but raindrops interrupted. Before long they were jogging for the trailhead parking lot in a downpour. Drenched, but in good spirits, they dove into the car. As they pulled onto the country road Ray asked, "When will you release the podcast episode?"

"Three weeks at most. There's enough material to do a two-part series."

"Will it reach a lot of people?"

"To be honest, I once struggled to find subscribers. Took forever to build a loyal base. But then I got a boost from an unexpected quarter. You'll never believe who gave me my greatest endorsement."

"Who?"

"Dr. Seidman."

"You're joking."

"Well, partially. He was a guest on a popular medical podcast. Halfway through the episode he lost it and launched a withering attack against me. I was an example of all that was wrong with pseudo-science. What was the dated insult he used? Quack Pot!"

Ray smiled, recognizing Seidman's clumsy ridicule.

"Best recommendation I could have received. My subscriber base quadrupled. I've become a hero to all those who have been ridiculed by the likes of Seidman. Fans set up a group called the Quack Pots."

"I hope you sent him a thank you card."

"I thank him almost every episode. It sounds silly, but the dust-up gave people the courage to call into my show. You know, people who had been afraid to speak up."

"Trust me, I know. He canceled funding for a project I spent years developing."

"I remember that story from the tea ceremony."

"I've been meaning to do a little research on the guy—to figure out what makes him tick. But I've been busy planning the wedding and getting ready for the baby."

"I've done more than enough research," Les said with a good-natured smirk.

"What's his deal?"

"Man writes more long-winded research papers than anyone could read in a lifetime. Tedious accounts of brain-damage cases. He quotes neuroscientists who fashion dubious claims based on brain abnormality—"

"Like Phineas Gage?"

"Oh, my, he adores the story of Phineas Gage encountering a brain-piercing railroad spike. He argues the case proves the brain is equivalent to consciousness. If brain damage impairs function, that's sufficient proof to declare the non-existence of spirit. If autistic kids can't recognize their mothers, their malfunction proves the non-existence of spirit. If surgically separated brain hemispheres change behavior, only material causes exist. No supernatural causes are possible."

"Typical materialist argument."

"Yes, but he goes further. Essentially, he argues that men are robots who only need correct programming to function in an optimum manner. But he means optimum for society, not for the individual. Furthermore, he insists that control of the programming should be centralized in the hands of a small number of technocrats."

"Doesn't surprise me," Ray said. "Explains his authoritarian bent."

"And of course, there's the personal side of the equation."

"Like?"

"At his previous hospital, he was accused of improper conduct. The results of the ethics review were sealed. Though he never received a formal reprimand, he soon resigned his post and moved across the country to accept the position he currently holds."

"Wonderful."

"Oh, I almost forgot. Would you consider speaking at a little gathering I'm hosting next month? Share your experience with a few people."

"A few?"

"A couple hundred of my best friends show up on a good day."

Ray scanned the rain-soaked meadows stretching out toward the mountains. He was a lousy public speaker. But, if he planned to take this new venture seriously, he would have to take an active role.

Les took Ray's reflective silence as a rejection. He had figured there would be no reply when Ray said, "I'll do it. But I have a request."

Les frowned. "Okay. What?"

"Hold the event at the new retreat. The one we built with James."

"Sounds good. You won't regret it."

27

The Front Range Spiritual Retreat turned out to be more than James, or anyone else, had dreamed.

The majestic pine lodge was a venue for all manner of gatherings, which included the planning meetings for the revised Changes in Action program. The community center also included a studio where Les had recently set up his podcast production. Father McCarty had an office, where he offered special direction. Pediatric patients of James by the dozens enjoyed access to a massive playroom. The heart of the lodge was the Great Hall that also served as a dining room.

However, in many cases, guests found the landscaped grounds to be most inviting. Gazebos decorated the rolling landscape. Meditation grottos nestled into granite outcroppings framed the stream's wandering path. Most visitors frequented the multiple prayer gardens. A sprawling picnic area at the front of the lodge formed a natural amphitheater.

The outdoor amphitheater was the center of activity on this festive day, a celebration of the release of Les Crane's new book, *The Spirit Hypotheses*. Ray was the scheduled keynote speaker; it would be the first time he would speak in a public forum about his near death experience.

"You ready?" Chase asked.

"I suppose. Though it's shaping up to be a bit of a circus," Ray noted. He pulled out his notes and adjusted the microphone clipped to his lapel as they made their way behind the makeshift dais.

"Take a deep breath. You'll do fine," Chase added.

"I know. I know."

They found Les conferring with the sound mixer. James looked on, a pleased and gracious host. Les presented Ray with a gift: an "official" pink unicorn lapel pin. Ray fastened the iconic pin to his lapel—with Bren capturing the moment for social media. She was dressed in the maid-of-honor gown she had worn on every important occasion since the wedding.

"You get a unicorn and I don't?" Bren complained.

"Did someone forget you? Hey, Les, how about a unicorn pin for a very important person."

Les tossed Bren a pin.

"And, Ray," Les said. "I forgot to mention… I arranged for you to have company on stage today. A fellow named Kyle Winston will interview you. Bright fellow. Physicist."

"Hold on. A physicist? I agreed to share an intimate story with a crowd of strangers. But I didn't plan to debate. We may need to cancel…"

Chase, sensing impending verbal fireworks, corralled Bren. "Hey, sweetie, let's go find a seat."

"Don't worry," Les said. "Kyle isn't here to trash your

account. He's an old friend. You'll like him. You can count on a friendly audience. They're all seeking answers. And they're more concerned about what's in their heads than what's in yours."

"So Kyle-the-physicist is a friend?"

"One of the best." Les climbed the steps to the dais. "Follow me," he shouted over his shoulder.

Ray followed and took his place on stage next to a heavyset man with a full gray beard and a thick pair of glasses. The stranger looked up at Ray and nodded before resuming work on his handwritten notes.

Though Ray trusted Les, this felt a lot like a betrayal.

"Kyle Winston?" Ray asked.

"That's the name. You must be Ray Carte. My pleasure," the physicist said, shaking Ray's hand.

"Do you prefer Kyle or Professor Winston?"

"Most of my students call me Professor K. They claim I'm kryptonite when it comes to their grade point average."

"Is this your first debate on the near-death experience?"

"Oh no," Kyle chuckled. "Been debating my entire academic career. Occasionally this topic comes up."

"Spectacular."

"But we're not debating. I'm genuinely interested in your experience. I believe you can help me fine tune a few theories."

"Glad to help," Ray responded, unable to quash a hint of sarcasm.

Les stepped to the podium and kicked off the event with his opening remarks.

Ray barely listened. He was too busy scanning the audience, trying to guess who was sympathetic and who was antagonistic, who was friend and who was foe. His prior dust-up with Seidman had left him jumpy when it came to sharing his experience. But then he spotted Hal screening arrivals at the entrance and was comforted. Knowing that he had a friendly bouncer on guard at the gate, Ray turned his attention back to Les.

"The first Spirit Hypothesis postulates a composite of body, mind, and spirit. These are components we can identify and separate. Paranormal researchers find this separation occurs during the near-death experience, the NDE."

Ray nodded agreement.

"Out-of-body perceptions—in which consciousness separates from the body—have been well documented. But the question remains: can we conduct experiments in a controlled setting that induce separation? I believe we can."

Ray admired Les' dedication and passion. Les had never experienced near death, yet he was dogged in his pursuit of the truth. He saw himself as a truth teller driven to awaken the scientific community. He possessed the drive that had always inspired scientists to explore the frontiers.

Les continued: "Science must become familiar with spiritual practices that separate soul from body. These practices have existed since the beginning of civilization."

Ray smiled as he watched Eva admonish Bren to stop fiddling with her Pink Unicorn pin. It meant a lot to Bren to be an official group member. And then, for a brief moment, Ray locked eyes with his mother. She tried hard to conceal her boredom.

He recalled the moment in the hospital before he had "returned" when he "viewed" Randi lower her head in prayer as she sat hopeless next to his failing body. In that moment, he had wanted nothing more than to comfort her. He had wanted to play the game of life once again. Now he had his chance. Taking a deep breath, he listened to Les expound his theory.

"My second hypothesis states 'the soul is the seat of consciousness.' The body, as lovely as some might be—"

The crowd broke into laughter.

"The body is strictly a stimulus-response machine. Consciousness is a property of the soul. And the mind is the interface between soul and physical body."

Though a few isolated coughs broke out in the audience, Les continued, undaunted.

"The third hypothesis states that the mind, along with the soul, separates from the body." Les waited a beat for the idea to sink in. "When the soul is released from the mortal vessel, it retains its memories. We say that a person, or a soul, experiences a post-mortem continuity of consciousness. When you die, you continue to be *you*. And you possess the potential to recall your past."

Ray understood that Les had created a set of interwoven hypotheses that could be subjected to testing. This set a high bar for anyone who summarily dismissed the existence of spirit. The carefully crafted set of hypotheses undermined ad hoc attacks based on false assertions. Instead, his critics would now have to address the claims set out before them.

"A very long time ago," Les continued. "Plato wrote that we

live as if we are trapped inside a cave. We observe shadows cast on the walls by light streaming in from outside. Our reality is a shadow reality. Tonight I have the honor of presenting a man who strayed outside the cave. Please welcome Ray Carte."

Ray stood and greeted the audience. He had not expected his legs would feel so weak. *A slight case of the nerves*, he noted. He scanned the sea of faces. *Who did he think he was to be lecturing about the great mysteries?*

Bren jumped up and documented the big moment. *Not now, Bren.*

"I'd like to thank the paparazzi for being here tonight," Ray joked, regaining control of his confidence.

Laughter rippled through the crowd. Ray took his seat as Les continued introductions. "And we're honored to be joined by Kyle Winston, all around Big Thinker. Professor K, as some call him, will interview Ray and help us understand what might be taking place."

A raucous contingent of Kyle's undergrad and graduate physics students cheered and hooted. Professor K was obviously well loved. Ray made a mental note: it would be unwise to upset or disrespect their hero professor.

"Ray, you were involved in an accident that resulted in an unusual experience," Kyle said.

"Yes, a near-death experience. If I had been in this audience two years ago, I would have shouted out, 'Fraud.' I would've scoffed. But that wreck changed my life. It tore apart my body, and also reordered my entire understanding of the world."

Ray found the initial response welcoming. He went on to recount his meeting with Alice as though talking to his extended family over Thanksgiving dinner. It helped that Kyle's enthusiasm for the subject was infectious.

"Are Plato's insights still applicable today?"

"I think so. We wander in a shadowy cave," Ray responded. "We've lost our way. A few people search for the way out. A few try to understand where we are, and where we've been. They seek to chart mankind's spiritual history. However, most stumble in the dark like robots leading a mechanical existence, devoid of meaning and purpose."

Ray had successfully engaged the audience and felt emboldened. "I've never been afraid of death, and never needed to invent a myth to deny death. I've no idea what good that would do. But, I also don't need to create a myth that dismisses the afterlife. Rather I must share what I observed. Maybe my story will help others construct a map that will lead us out of the cave."

Kyle picked up the thread. "Ray's account fits perfectly with the hypothesis Les stated: our consciousness exists distinct from objects, energy, process. Dualism should never have been abandoned as the model. Do you agree, Ray?"

"Yes. Years ago, another Professor K brought these same ideas to my attention. At the time, I was not sufficiently humble to grasp his view."

One of Kyle's students spoke up, pressing the skeptic's viewpoint. "But don't you agree that the human mind is notoriously unreliable, that we can easily be deluded and fooled by our perceptions?"

The crowd murmured nervously: the fireworks had begun.

The intense student continued. "Don't you agree there is only one way to describe what happened and that is by observing the brain?"

Kyle interjected, "No I don't agree. Neither does our guest. That's not how we observe consciousness. While Ray's experience does not, by itself, definitively establish the existence of spirit, it is a very important start. It provides us with a direction for research."

"I'm what researchers call raw evidence," Ray chimed in. My observations would have been impossible had I not actually been separate from the body. My body was in one location while I observed events in a different location. That's simply raw data."

Les took up the argument. "Ray's experience may not prove the case, but it punches holes in the materialist argument. It forces us to consider alternate models of reality."

The skeptical student was not about to concede. "But that's assuming we believe his version of events. That's assuming he's a credible witness."

"Previously, I would have been the last person to accept an out-of-body experience as valid," Ray responded.

"We appreciate your skepticism," said Les. "But do not arbitrarily malign this man's credibility. Many people would vouch for Mr. Carte's character."

The audience broke into polite applause.

The chagrined student apologized. "Professor K, I'm sorry. I was out of line. Yet we know that consciousness emerges from the aggregate neuronal activity of the brain. That is scientific consensus, which is better than speculation. After all, if we let Mr. Carte decide what he experienced, we might as well let everyone decide."

Ray was ready with a rebuttal. "I described my direct experience. I did not engage in wild conjecture about my brain, conjecture that no one can ever observe. Why should we replace direct observation with conjecture? Who does that? Those who listen to my account can make up their own minds and undertake their own research."

"But that leaves us with nothing but opinions," the determined student replied.

Les met the challenge. "There's no evidence that consciousness emerges from brain cells. Zero. But we have ample evidence that consciousness exists separate from a body. There are traditions thousands of years old that train people to observe states of consciousness. This is actually very old science."

The student was about to interrupt once again but Kyle signaled for his silence.

Les continued. "In our search to understand the near-death experience we can turn to revered traditions. In addition, there's a significant body of testimony regarding the near-death state. This evidence, collected over thousands of years, tells us there's a great deal more to the story than modern science admits."

Kyle added to the argument. "In spite of a lingering strain of skeptical materialism, in our field we have moved on to new theories. As quantum field theory has matured, we have begun to realize the vital role that observers play in the emergence of reality. Some even speculate that observation plays a role in the collapse of the wave function."

"What the heck is that?" Les asked, mystified.

A smattering of students chuckled at his playful show of ignorance.

"Imagine a set of probabilities that describe all possible observable outcomes that might emerge from a quantum field. These probabilities quantify what *might* happen."

"So these equations might describe the possible results if one rolled dice."

"A little like that. Eventually, the dice are rolled and one set of numbers show up. We go from probability to an actual event. Out of a huge number of possible outcomes reality springs forth. That is what we call the collapse of the wave function."

"So some speculate our mind affects the ultimate result?" Ray asked.

"Some put forth the theory that conscious observers—like you and you and you—help determine how probabilities collapse into an actual reality."

Ray spotted Bren rolling her eyes at the physics talk. She mimed becoming dizzy and falling off her chair. This covered her escape up the aisle and away from the weighty dialogue.

Ray admired her precocious demeanor. He was tempted to follow her.

Meanwhile, Kyle continued his impromptu classroom lecture. "This theory very much resembles the lessons Ray received. There's a fascinating overlap. We must remain open—"

"In short," Les interjected, "when it comes to the study of consciousness, some scientists are playing catch-up with spiritual traditions while others, sadly, have fallen hopelessly behind." Les addressed the skeptical student. "Thank you for your question, sir. Anyone else have a question?"

A bevy of hands shot up. An usher passed the microphone from the dissenter to another audience member.

"Mr. Carte, did you spend time looking at your body?" a woman asked.

Her question was greeted with a smattering of chuckles.

"Initially I had no desire to see what happened to the body. No desire to experience pain and suffering. I gained my freedom but lost my courage."

His response garnered additional laughter.

"When we enter that awkward state, the biggest challenge we face is confusion. Until that moment comes, we're very certain we're only a body. It is hard to let go of that illusion. We cling to our attachments."

$* * *$

A moment later a series of odd and quite unexpected events transpired.

An altercation arose at the front gate.

Ray squinted into the bright sunlight, struggling to discern the situation.

Hal, in his role as bouncer, shoved a guest past the gate and out of the event.

Ray wondered what the interloper could possibly have

done to anger Hal.

When he blocked the sun and viewed more clearly, he was shocked to discover the ejected guest was Dr. Seidman. *What nerve.* Obviously, he had crashed the gate intending to sabotage the event, just like he had sabotaged their funding.

But then something truly bizarre took place.

Bren skipped past Hal, holding the hand of a monk. The folds of his brown tunic, his quizzical smile, and his round, balding head were familiar: *It was the monk that had been Alice.* It was the monk who said: *Let us bring your confusion to a conclusion.*

Ray was certain he was hallucinating. Maybe the NDE experience was catching up and exacting an unexpected toll.

"You alright?" Kyle asked with concern.

"Yeah, I guess so—"

Kyle followed Ray's gaze…

Bren removed her pink unicorn pin and affixed it to Seidman's jacket lapel. And then she extended her hand in invitation. "If you join the club and respect the unicorn, you can come in."

The psychologist nodded his agreement. Tears seemed to well up in his eyes.

Bren took his hand and led him through the gate and into the crowd. His expression conveyed humble appreciation at a child's show of compassion. Bren had somehow helped him surmount a hurdle.

Hal had stepped aside, speechless. He turned to study the monk standing nearby, alone. The monk simply bowed and departed with a kindly wink. As he walked away he faded out of existence *like a ghost.*

Ray mumbled to no one in particular. "The lessons are never ending."

Contentment wrapped his mind in its comforting folds. "Better than alright," he said to Kyle.

Les had been oblivious to the skirmish. He brought his presentation to its natural close. "And on that note we'll transition to coffee and cake."

Ray gazed at Bren who kept Seidman firmly in tow. It appeared that an enemy had finally come to make peace. Ray figured the rest would be easy. He had survived his first public talk and was now ready, more than ever, to share his story, even with those who were hostile and skeptical.

He realized he had changed. He knew with certainty that the world was teeming with relationships and, if you focused too narrowly on your own concerns, you missed opportunities to reconcile and nurture those relationships. He knew at that moment that if he ever found himself on that mountain with Alice again, he did not want to arrive burdened with regret over how he had treated others.

He thought of his father, a man who had failed to deal with his emotions in this world. Now, beyond this life, he was forced to confront his demons. Ray felt only pity for him and released the seed of regret he had carried for too long. Yes, maybe, when he was a child, he might have reached out instead of nursing his wounded anger. But he was just a kid and lacked the benefit of the lessons. If he had possessed the lessons, he might have been able to help others heal.

In any event, the lessons he had learned beyond this life

prepared him to greet his own daughter who was soon to come into the world. He and Chase had already settled on a name: Alice.